A Werewolf for Christmas

Addison James

Addison James

Book Cover by K.B. Barrett Designs

Paperback ISBN: 979-8-9924452-7-5

To everyone who just needs someone who adores you and is eager to help you calm your anxious brain.

Contents

Content Notes

This book depicts an already-established relationship between a human and a werewolf. Max is two thousand years old, and therefore significantly older than Casey.

There are multiple scenes of fighting and violence on the page of this book, and Max remembers even more violence, including a vague discussion of harm and murder of children when he was a child. Max suffered an emotionally and physically abusive childhood.

Casey's family is emotionally abusive.

There are on-page depictions of an anxiety disorder.

This book includes several sexual scenes and is only for audiences 18+.

December 23rd, 6:30 am

I wake Casey up with my head between her thighs. It's the best way to start a morning, and I'm the lucky bastard who gets to be here, teasing her awake with my tongue.

Technically, my day started half an hour ago. I need less sleep than the average human, so I get to wake up and watch my woman sleep for a bit.

She's so damn soft when she's sleeping. She has these tiny, adorable little huffing noises, and her skin is warm and soft, and her mouth is always open just slightly. She usually sleeps in just her panties, and since I run hot as hell, our blankets are always kicked down by the time I wake up, leaving all that smooth, warm, inked skin on perfect display for me.

And that leaves me half an hour or so every morning to just drink in the sight of her. My Casey, my sweetheart, all soft and relaxed in bed. I'll trace her freckles, her tattoos, her curves, the wild mess of her dark curls, her long eyelashes laid so gently against her cheek, the gentle opening of her full lips.

1

I've woken up next to her a thousand times by now. Every morning, seeing her is like a revelation all over again.

And then it's time for her to wake up. Technically, she could start her work day whenever she wants, since she works from home and makes her own schedule. But she likes working a day similar to mine so we can have our evenings together.

My girl is so good to me.

So I'll tug down those cute little panties, and the most she ever does is roll a bit, maybe huff. Casey trusts me, even in her sleep, and I can't describe what that does to my heart.

And then I'll start my morning with the most important meal of the day: Casey's warm, wet cunt.

As hungry and desperate as I am for her, I make sure to start slow. I like when she wakes up like this, still soft as she slides from sleep to waking, her little huffs of welcome surprise making her lovely tits heave, the way her hand always slides to my hair, soft and slow, not quite pulling.

She doesn't disappoint this morning, either, making a "mmmm," sound as she slips into wakefulness, her legs briefly tightening around my head, her hand sliding into my hair, and my name on her lips. "Max."

It's a breath, barely audible even to someone like me, and yet it also makes me feel like the most powerful man alive. I suck at her clit with a little more pressure, then slide my hands up the back of her thighs, grabbing handfuls of that delicious, perfect ass to pull her closer to my face.

"Max!" she cries, louder now that I've switched from a languid tease to a more direct approach. I want to make her come. I'm starving, and only she can satisfy my craving.

Her grip on my hair tightens, a sure sign that she's just as hungry for it as I am. I've grown my hair longer in the last few years, just so she can get a better grip on me. There is absolutely nothing better than my woman steering me where she wants me.

"That's it," I murmur against her thigh, giving her a momentary break as she writhes against my face. "You're delicious, sweetheart, so fucking sexy like this, come for me—"

"Max," she whines, and I take that as my cue to get back to work.

I'm in heaven, hearing her whimpers and feeling her writhe against me, tasting her sweet honey on my tongue. Fuck. She's going to come soon; I can feel it. I pin her hips to my face, not letting her squirm away, holding her exactly where I want her.

When she comes, she moans my name, voice all breathless and sweet. She squeezes my hair involuntarily, holding me where she needs me, like I'd ever willingly leave my place between her thighs. I lap up every drop, desperate for her, and don't back off until she makes that little noise she does when she's too oversensitive.

"Good morning, sweetheart," I murmur, pressing kisses against her stomach, letting my hands move up to squeeze at her waist. I can't let her go, can't keep my mouth to myself. Not when I could worship her instead.

Her fingers trace through my hair, scratching lightly at my scalp as I reach her sternum tattoo, kissing along the lattice of flowers there. "Good morning," she says, her voice deliciously rough. "Are you going to let me take care of you, now?"

"You think the taste of your sweet cunt doesn't take care of me, baby?" I ask, nipping at the underside of her breast. "Casey, you're so fucking perfect."

She flushes, and it travels from the tips of her ears down to her chest, and I have to hide my smile between her tits. My girl likes praise, and she deserves so goddamn much of it.

"Max," she nearly whines, tugging at my hair now.

"Yes, sweetheart?"

"Let me get you off."

"Whatever the lady wants." I rise so I'm hovering over her, propping myself up on my hands and knees. "Can I fuck you, sweetheart? All slow and deep like you need it, my beautiful girl?"

Her breath hitches again. "Please."

"Your wish is my command." I reposition myself so my cock presses against her cunt. Casey is never a demanding person, so it's a point of pride that I can make her so horny that she gets pushy. Right now, she wraps those wonderfully thick, inked thighs around my hips, pulling me closer, impatient and demanding.

"So fucking hot," I tell her, and then push inside her.

She groans, her head falling back against the pillows, her eyes sliding shut. I pull back out and thrust in, deep and hard even as I take my time. It causes a ripple to move through her body, first shaking those delicious thighs, then her rounded belly, and then finally her beautiful tits.

If there is a heaven, this is it, right here. Casey, letting me bring her pleasure, warm and wet and soft around me, moaning with her head thrown back against the pillows as her thighs try to pin me to her. A man could never ask for more.

Without losing pace, I kiss her, hard and desperate and hungry for her. Once upon a time she would have objected, saying she had morning breath. But that was long ago. Now she knows I'll do anything for just a second of her time, that I'm starving for her, and that morning breath doesn't even register.

Five days ago, I was knuckle deep inside her cunt while she bled all over my hand, and it was far from the first time I'd eased period cramps with orgasms. I think I've finally convinced her I want her any which way, whenever, forever, and that there's not a single moment where I'm not hungry for her.

I keep kissing her, insistent and demanding everything she has to give me. Then I move to kiss her jaw, wanting her mouth free so I can listen to those delicious moans as I drive her higher again.

I am so fucking close to the edge. I always am around her, so it's not a surprise. Pushing back the orgasm is painful, but I'll be damned if I come before she does. I need her tight cunt to milk my cock before I can spill inside her.

"You're so fucking perfect for me, sweetheart," I murmur, moving so I can whisper the words directly in her ear. I catch the helix piercing with my tongue, flicking it lightly.

My thrusts have gone slow, more grinding into her than actually thrusting, but that's okay. I know without having to ask that I'm grinding against her clit just right, her moans taking on a higher, more desperate edge.

"So pretty when you come," I continue. "You going to be a good girl and come for me, Casey? Going to be sweet and give me what I need?"

It's like she stops breathing for a moment, her whole body going completely still before she comes apart, her cunt squeezing my cock like she's worried I'd ever actually willingly pull out of her. I can't resist a moment longer, filling her and biting at her neck while I do.

I rock into her helplessly for a minute, lost in the feel of her, in the pleasure sapping all my senses. When I can breathe again, I pause, holding my hips perfectly still, giving her the filled stretch she likes without any additional stimulation that might overwhelm her.

"You're so fucking good to me," I groan, easing my upper body back so I can see her face, blissed out and relaxed. If I didn't know better, I'd think she was planning on falling back asleep. "Everything I could have ever dreamed of—did it feel good for you, sweetheart?" I ask her.

"You know it did," she murmurs, looking at me with a smile so soft it makes my heart ache.

Yeah, I know it did. I know precisely how to make my woman fall apart around me. I've studied her and her every reaction, and I know exactly what makes her come. "Perfect girl," I tell her.

She squirms a bit in the way that tells me she needs me to pull out soon. I slip out of her, pulling back enough to watch some of my come slip out of her. I resist the urge to push it back in—she's oversensitive, and right before we both go to work isn't the time to start something that might take hours to truly finish—and instead lean down to kiss her sweetly.

She kisses me back, and just when I'm thinking fuck work and that we can spend all day here, she pushes lightly at my chest, her fingernails digging in slightly as she pushes. I hope she leaves marks. "Go shower," she murmurs, blinking contentedly at me as she smiles. "I'll get breakfast for both of us."

I'd like to drag her into the shower, but Casey is always conscious of time; she'd never want to inconvenience someone by being late. So I nod, steal one more quick kiss, and go to clean myself up.

I wash off in a barely warmed shower—Casey takes showers the temperature of the sun, and they always smell so fucking good with her body wash and shampoo on the steamy air, but without her here I just want to be in and out as quick as I can—and then find a set of office clothes to pull on.

Office clothes. It's a ridiculous pretension, and often entirely impractical in my line of work. But it's necessary for keeping up the lie, both with Casey and with the general human public.

Because I work for the fucking governor, so surely I have to wear fucking slacks and a blazer and these damn shiny shoes. That's what the world needs to see. Never mind that there's a not-insignificant chance that the clothes will have blood on them by the end of the night; all that matters is that I look the part.

When I finally emerge downstairs, Casey is just finishing plating eggs, wearing nothing but the tiny, flimsy little pink robe that makes me absolutely feral for her.

It's partially open, and as she turns, I can confirm that she didn't even bother to pull her panties back on, which means she's just wearing this insignificant, nearly transparent robe and is dripping my come down her thighs.

Fuck. Me.

"Thank you for breakfast, sweetheart," I say, and I think I do a good job at disguising how fucking desperate I am for her again.

Her smile is a little wicked though, something that's just for me and tells me she absolutely knows what she's doing to me. "Coffee is on the table," she tells me.

"You're too good for me," I say, then grab her around the waist one-handed and drag her to the table. If left to her own devices, she'll keep assigning herself chores instead of eating.

I put the plate she handed me in front of her, then go to the stove to plate up a second one, grabbing her half-drained coffee mug and refilling it just the way she likes it before walking back over.

"Will I see you at lunch today?" she asks.

I try to get home for lunch most every day. Thankfully, Casey hasn't yet asked why a supposedly busy gubernatorial staffer can get two hour long lunches most days. "I'm going to try," I tell her, because I don't like making promises I'm not sure if I can keep. I better be able to fucking come home, though. It's two days until Christmas, and that might not mean a lot to creatures like me, but I'll be damned if I let Luc interfere with my time with my girl.

"I'm taking the afternoon off," she reminds me. "So I can get the shopping done."

"Give me half your list," I tell her. "Or better yet, give me the whole thing. You don't need to worry about that."

She bites her lip, clearly tempted, but shakes her head. "It'll be good for me," she murmurs. "To, you know, be out there."

I consider her for a long moment, and she holds my gaze the entire time.

Casey doesn't like crowds. They overwhelm her, making her brain go into overdrive and her body feel out of her control. That's how we met—I didn't expect anyone else to be going to the gym at two in the morning, but Casey prefers off-peak times, where the risk of running into a crowd is lower.

Well, that's not precisely true. Creatures like me don't really need to work out, and I hadn't intended to walk into that twenty-four-hour gym that night. I'd been following a target on Luc's orders when I'd seen the curvy, tattooed goddess walking into that gym and completely lost my train of thought.

The target had gotten away, at least for that night, and I'd gotten a new gym membership and a carefully thought out plan for introducing myself to Casey that I'd immediately flubbed, unable to even remotely keep my cool around her. Thankfully, she'd given me a chance, anyway.

But the point is, Casey doesn't like crowds. And she does online therapy for it, and I've been told that I over accommodate her, and that I need to help support her in pushing herself when she feels safe. So I've been trying. That doesn't mean that I think going out grocery shopping two days before Christmas is an ideal plan.

Casey is so damned strong. I have every confidence she can do anything she puts her mind to. I just worry about the cost later, because I have no doubt there will be one. Yes, she'll be able to do the grocery shopping, but when she gets home, will she be able to relax?

She's made herself sick before, and she has such big plans for Christmas. I don't want her to lose out on them, not when her family coming over tomorrow night will already be hard enough.

I consider for a long moment, trying to find the best option so I can support her. If she wants to try this, then I'm not going to stop her, but I'm damn sure going to give her every bit of help that I can. "Can I come with you?"

"You have work," she reminds me, adding more pepper to her eggs.

"C'mon, baby, it's two days until Christmas. Half the government is closed down today. I'm sure they'll be fine."

Maybe human governments don't run on major holidays, but for creatures like me, Christmas is just any other day. I've never taken the day off before I met Casey, but now, I'll insist on every moment I can get with her. I'm going to be around and give Casey every fucking thing she wants for Christmas.

She smiles softly, seemingly unsure. "I'd like that," she admits. "If you can. Don't worry if you can't."

Men like me are dangerous, and Luc is absolutely aware of this fact. He knows you don't antagonize the animals, especially not the ones who can snap your head off. He'll give me the damn afternoon off, and the rest of the week off, too.

"I'll meet you for lunch," I tell her, leaning across the table to kiss her. She tastes like that peppermint creamer she's been adding to her coffee for the past three weeks. "And then we'll go get whatever you need for tomorrow."

I steal another kiss, finish my eggs, and then head out. I need to check in with Luc.

When I drive, I force myself to let go of the version of me that exists only when I'm in our house. Another version of me exists in the outside world, and that's the version Luc and the others expect to see.

I'm not a good man, never have been, and don't pretend to be except when I'm with Casey. Even then, I'm not really a good man—I can't ever pretend I wouldn't do horrible, horrible things if I needed to keep her happy and healthy and alive—but at least I'm a good husband.

I'm not technically her husband, no matter how much I want to be, but it doesn't stop me thinking about myself like that. I'll be the best damn husband for Casey.

In the entire time I've known her, there's only been four things she's wanted that I've denied her, and each one hurts me bitterly. I want to give her the world, and each of these things is something I ache to give her, but just can't.

One, a pet. Casey has never flat-out asked if we could get a pet at our place, but I'd have to be blind to not see the way she coos at cute animals. She strikes me as a cat person—or perhaps I just want to be the only canine in her life—and I could see her working from home with a cute little cat curled up on her lap.

I'd take her to the shelter this afternoon to adopt one, but animals don't like me much. They're much more astute than humans at sensing the predator inside me, and how would I explain that to Casey? A whole shelter going quiet when I walk in, all the animals too afraid to be near me, and then whatever fluffy little creature she adopts spending its life hiding away from me, terrified to be in my presence. I can't do that to her.

Two, a vacation. I travel plenty on Luc's orders, but I've never taken Casey away for more than a night or two. I've had wet dreams of her and me at some tropical resort, her in some little string bikini that shows off her tits, me rubbing sunblock into her skin. But if Luc needs me, I need to be here. That's

13

the deal I made, and I can't see that debt being discharged in this lifetime.

Three, a tattoo. Casey has a whole body full of them, beautiful artwork she takes so much pride in. And she knows I love them and can spend hours touching and licking them. There's a crescent moon on her upper thigh that I can get hard at just the barest sight of, like some Pavlovian reaction.

She knows I have a few tattoos, too, so she doesn't understand why I won't go meet her favorite artist—a nice woman named Jack who I did a very thorough background check on the first time I learned she was going to be putting her hands on my wife—but how do I explain that, in order for a tattoo to stick in my skin for more than a day or so, the ink needs to be infused with silver dust? And that the tattoos I have are more than six centuries old?

Four is the hardest, though. I know Casey wants to be married. We've even talked about it, and in the last six months or so she's started to say things like *when we're married*, which makes me feel simultaneously like I'm fifteen feet tall and like I'm shit on her shoe.

I can't marry her. Not when I can't give her the truth. And I can't give her the truth until I can give her a solution. What, am I supposed to say hey, I'm a supernatural creature, I turn into a great big dog sometimes, I strike fear into the hearts of nearly everyone, I can lift a car one-handed, and, oh yeah, I stopped aging when Roman legions were still in style?

14

Worse, though, is I know what's expected after a marriage. Children. I suppose I could pretend that I don't want them, but Casey would know I was a liar. A baby that's half her sounds like the best thing in the world, but I just know it would be like me. A baby like me could kill her. It'd be like having a wild animal in the house.

So I can't marry her. Not until I can promise us both that I have a solution to that little problem.

Either a solution that makes me mortal like her, or one that makes her like me. I'm not going to be picky about it, although I won't lie; I'd prefer to make her immortal. For one thing, I think this world could use someone like Casey sticking around a lot longer than one measly human lifetime. For another, I'm not sure if I believe in any sort of specific afterlife, but if I did, I'd be an idiot to think people like Casey and people like me go to the same one. And I can't find it in me to be satisfied with just a few decades of her.

And that's why I have to go see Luc, even if it's two days until Christmas and there's nothing I want more than to do whatever is on Casey's honey-do list for this party tomorrow night.

I owe Luc my life. I owe Luc my soul, really, because the compound we'd been raised in, bred and trained as soldiers, caged until it was time to fight, was no life at all. Luc had been the only one smart enough to find a way out, and he'd chosen to take me with him. In return, he'd asked for just one little thing; my protection and dedication to his rise to power.

It had taken just about two millennia, but I'd done it. I'd helped him secure a metaphorical crown, been the muscle behind his empire. I'd intimidated, threatened, stalked, and murdered on his behalf.

I'd even fucking hammered in lawn signs when he decided he needed to run for governor, just to have that one extra layer of political power. Because it wasn't enough to rule creatures like us from the shadows; he'd needed to have the real, tangible power that even the humans can see.

Lucius Lawson is going to be President of the United States one day, a hilarious fate for a man who is not technically a US citizen and is far, far older than the country in question. And for a while, that hadn't bothered me at all, because I'd assumed I'd be out. I'd have facilitated his rise to power, given him the control he needed, and I'd either be working for him of my own free will, or else moving on.

Until I'd met Casey.

I'd just cleared one debt to Luc when I already knew I'd need to enter into another one; I needed whatever magic there was to make our lifespans match. I didn't care what it would take, or who I'd need to kill. I just needed it. And I know I'm not smart enough to find it for myself. But Luc is.

So yeah, I'm not a good man. Luc's orders have permanently stained my hands red, and I won't pretend I could ever

16

be clean of them. I won't pretend I care that much, either. But for Casey? I'll be whatever she fucking needs. I'll be Luc's killer to the rest of the world, and the husband who adores her whenever we're together.

December 23rd, 9:00am

"**M**aximus!" Bartholomew is another one of Luc's acolytes. I don't even think he's under coercion to be here. I also think he creamed his jeans when Luc announced we were launching a political campaign. "How's the wife? Ready for Christmas?"

I tense, because I never know what to do when Casey is brought up here. I needed to tell them about her. I had to re-sell my soul to Luc for a chance with her, after all. I also needed to make it perfectly fucking clear that she is entirely off-limits, and that if something should happen to me, every person in this building will do everything in their power to give her whatever she needs, up to and including laying down their lives for her.

It helps to be Luc's oldest surviving soldier, with a history soaked in the legends of people I've killed for him. No one fucks with me and mine.

"Casey's fine," I grunt. Casey is amazing, and Casey is trying to go shopping two days before Christmas, and Casey is going to try to mend bridges with her family tomorrow, and Casey looks at me in a way that turns my heart to absolute putty, and I think her smile is the best thing I've ever experienced in my entire damn life. I'm not telling him any of that. "Is Luc in?"

"For an hour now."

"Can I see him?" Better to ask, especially when I want something.

"He asked to see you when you get in."

That is ominous as hell, but it's not unexpected, given my job. It does mean that someone is probably going to die today, but that's nothing new.

But goddamn, why does it have to be today?

I open his office door, automatically sweeping the space before looking over at Luc, who's faking being busy behind the ostentatious desk.

"I need this afternoon off," I say without any greeting. Some people might think it's rude, but I think a couple thousand years and a mountain of corpses earn me the ability to talk to Luc however I want. I consider, then add, "And the next two days, too," just to make sure my abruptness isn't overlooked.

"I can't." He doesn't even look up when he says it.

"Bullshit. Send Bartholomew to do your dirty work." Or any of a half dozen others. They might not be me, but they

19

can surely hold down the fort for a few days. We were all raised to be killers, after all.

"You'll want this one, Max."

Luc isn't a big guy. He was always the runtiest wolf in the litter when we were growing up, and he never really did catch up to the rest of us. A well-tailored suit can do a lot, but it can't hide that.

Even so, he positively radiates power. Luc is a force of nature, destructive without being malicious and absolutely, unquestionably, in control of every situation. I wouldn't want to cross him any more than I would a forest fire.

Of course, I'm usually the one who lights the fires for him, so the situation is a little different between us.

I sigh, knowing I won't escape until I give in. "Why do I want this one, Luc?"

"First off, how's Casey?"

I suppress the shudder. There's not much that can truly get to me, but every time Luc says Casey's name, I can barely hide how bothered I am. They've only met once, and Casey spent the five days between getting the dinner invite and the actual dinner freaking the fuck out because "we're going to have dinner with the governor, and what if I say something weird or spill food or just look like an idiot?" I'd done everything in my power to soothe those concerns, and decidedly not mentioned that she was worried for all the wrong reasons.

Lucius Lawson doesn't care if she says something awkward. But he's a cold, calculating son-of-a-bitch, and I doubt he's ever looked at another person in his entire life and not come up with a plan about how he can use them.

Casey works as perfect leverage to keep my loyalty, but I don't doubt Luc could find another use for her, and I shudder to think what it could be.

So I hate him talking about her, but I can't avoid it. "We're having a dinner party tomorrow. She's busy planning it."

"And you didn't invite me," he scolds. I think he's aiming at being playful.

"Her family is coming. There'll be enough tension in that house," I say flatly. "Why do I want this one, Luc?"

"I asked about Casey because I made you a promise," he says, pushing some papers aside before he fully looks up at me. "And I keep my word, Max. So you're going to want this, even if it means missing your little dinner party."

I freeze. "Spell it out for me," I say, needing to know exactly what this means.

"I have word on Alexander," he says. "And he's yours, if you want him. And if you bring him back to me after."

Alexander. The man who made creatures like Luc and I, who made every one of the creatures Luc has collected over the centuries.

When we were young, we thought he was a god. He might as well have been, with how our entire lives were forced to center around him and his orders. His power could end our worlds as we knew them.

Now, we assume he must be some sort of sorcerer, something with a potent knowledge of arcane arts. Someone who can turn boys into wolves, and spiders, and bears, and a hundred other deadly creatures. We never found out if we were born this way, if it was something he did to us in the womb, or if it was something he did to us shortly after, but all I know is my memories were of being raised in a litter, a wolf pup who sometimes was a human, and who was bred for war.

And I remember Alexander doling out pain and punishment and magic so terrifying it made us weep in fear.

I haven't seen him since the day Luc offered me a way out. I've killed monsters in my time, but I've never particularly wanted to go after Alexander. Some monsters were meant to stay in the past.

"What does that have to do with Casey?" I ask. My voice is raspy and I hate it, but I can't squash the memories entirely.

"Who else in the entire world would know how to make your girl immortal? And you're not a kid anymore, Max. At this point, I think it's fair to say even Alexander should be scared of you. Beat the answer out of him." He smiles at me. His smile is so cold that I can't imagine how he ever got elected to office. Surely even the humans can see what a scary motherfucker Luc is. "What do you say, Max?"

What do I say? I say this is the only chance I've ever heard of, and it's also the worst option I could think of. And he has terrible timing, too.

But that is what it is. Life works like that, and I can't afford to pass this opportunity up. I'll do whatever it takes to have a forever with Casey.

"I'm in."

The cold smile only gets wider. "Good. Send Bartholomew in, will you? I have a job for him."

December 23rd, 10:30 am

I'm expecting Luc's lead to be some sort of underground fighting ring of werewolf puppies, or perhaps mutant alligator children living in the sewer. But no, instead it's a shop that sells herbs.

The shop is run out of a two-story home, with a faded sign hammered crookedly into the front yard announcing Herbs and Remedies are sold there. There's an arrow pointing to the side door, so that's the door I knock on with perhaps more force than necessary.

The place doesn't smell like the herb aisle of the grocery store. It doesn't smell like an old-fashioned apothecary, either. The stench of magic is positively stifling.

Luc might recruit creatures like him and I, those who are made into this, bred as little baby monsters, but we're not the only supernatural creatures in the world. I would have been more than happy to practice live-and-let-live with them, but that had never been Luc's mission.

He'd wanted every demon, every sorcerer, every vampire and warlock and half-witted hedge witch under his thumb. And then, when even that wasn't enough, he'd gone for the humans, too.

Neither world had ever really wanted us. We're not human, even if I suspect we all had human parents. The human world would never take us, not if they knew the truth. The supernatural world wanted us, but in the worst possible way. They'd bred us to be their monsters.

Luc told me millennia ago that if they wanted monsters, then they could reap what they sowed, and we've lived by that ever since.

I let a disdainful look fall over my face when I hear footsteps on the other side of the door. The door opens a crack to reveal a man leaning hard into the wizardry stereotype, with a bushy white beard and eyebrows and not a strand of hair on his head. "Oh—I—I've been expecting you."

"Open the door." Cold. Precise. Leaving no room for argument, because there is no room when I'm like this. You either do what I say, or you die. It's been that simple since the day Luc gave me my first assignment.

He opens the door, and I step inside. The smell of magic is worse here, and I take a cursory look around. I already know there's no one else here—my senses could detect that from outside the shop—so I know this isn't an ambush, and he's not hiding Alexander underneath the table. The place is filled with haphazard bins and jars, half of which are full and half of which are empty, stacked up near a work station where he likely mixes custom blends.

Most of the herbs are unrecognizable to me. But one in the corner I can recognize from scent alone. It's chamomile. Casey's therapist recommended drinking a tea made from the stuff, so sometimes our house smells like it when she's especially anxious.

A shame this guy here sold to Alexander. If I wasn't here for work, maybe I'd pick up some tea for Casey.

"The sorcerer was here?" I ask.

He swallows, and his fear is almost strong enough to drown out the scent of magic. "Y-yes. Yesterday. I called the number as soon as he left," he says defensively.

I never knew that Luc had been directing people to do that, but then again, not my department. It raises the question how long he's been looking for Alexander, though. What the fuck does he want from him? I can't delude myself into thinking that he's truly doing this just for me.

"Tell me everything."

He tells me what he already told Luc, but I make him repeat every detail. A sorcerer, tall and rail thin with pale skin and dark hair, youthful and with a scar from left eye to chin, came in with a very specific order. The shop owner rattles off a list, then offers to write it down, which I accept. The shop owner had apparently tried to make small talk, asking what he planned to use the herbs for. I can't decide if this was brave or stupid, but either way, he didn't get an answer. He'd had all the herbs on hand, so none needed to be custom-ordered, which unfortunately means Alexander doesn't need to come back to pick them up.

"If you tell anyone I was here, I'll kill you," I tell him, voice low. I don't need fancy threats. People know I'm serious on sight now. "If he comes back, you call immediately." He nods rapidly. "And one more thing."

"Anything," he squeaks.

"Did he touch anything?"

Werewolves aren't bloodhounds, but we do well enough. A hand-written receipt and a pen also aren't the greatest items to collect a scent from, but I can work with anything. If this is my one chance to find a way to tie my life to Casey's forever, then I'll do absolutely anything to take it.

And hell, if the herbs are essential to whatever the fuck Alexander does to make his immortals, maybe I'll come back and give this old man some business as a thank you for his trouble.

I check my watch. If I want to make it on time to lunch with Cascy, I need to start heading back towards our house.

Alexander has waited two thousand years for justice. He can wait a few hours more.

Our house is on a quieter, tree-lined street. It's a two story brick Colonial, the type of place someone might expect a rising political servant with some inherited wealth to own. Luc had ensured that.

Casey had protested that it was all way too much when I first moved her in. She'd argued that she couldn't cover her half of the mortgage. She'd worried she was taking advantage of me. But I've had centuries to make money, and Luc always ensures we have some. And he might have made me buy the house for appearances, but I've never loved anyplace more than this house since Casey moved in.

She's hung art on the walls, and put throw blankets on the couch. The house has four bedrooms, and ours smells so deliciously like her that I think I've died and gone to heaven when I'm lying in bed sometimes. One of the rooms is her office. Another one is my office, because I tell her I'm working from home sometimes, although truth be told I'm usually just playing solitaire on my computer, listening to her through the wall, because it's not like my work can be done from home, even if she doesn't know that. The fourth bedroom is a home gym, which might be another instance of me over-accommodating her anxiety, since the gym was one of the few places she went out to comfortably before we got together, but in my defense going to the gym at two in the morning is how murders happen.

I'd even put a pool in the backyard, because Casey likes to swim for her cardio when the weather is good enough, and I like her being happy and wearing damn sexy bathing suits that show off so much cleavage and ink.

This place is ours. Our stamp is all over it, and I always feel more relaxed just walking in the door.

Out there, I'm the monster Alexander made me and Luc needs me to be. In here, I'm Casey's man.

Right now, there's a Christmas wreath hanging on the front door, and when I walk in, the place smells like lemon cleaning products. Clearly, she did some work for the party before signing in for her workday.

And I'm the absolute asshole who is about to tell her I can't help later today. I promise myself that I'll make it up to her.

The flowers in my hand are a small start at that. I don't know if they'll clash with her holiday decorations for tomorrow, but if they do, she can hide them in our room during the party. Flowers always make her smile and blush so prettily, so I like to bring them whenever I can.

I move quietly through the house, looking for her. She's exactly where I expect, in her office all curled up in her chair, sitting with her legs under her in a way she swears is comfortable.

I groan at the sight. Since she works online and rarely needs to do video calls, she dresses comfortably when she works. During the hotter months, she wears these skimpy little silk shorts and tank tops that show off more skin than they cover. I can come home and find my favorite crescent moon tattoo on her thigh peeking out from those shorts, and have more than once gone to my knees under her desk as a result.

When it's colder outside, though, she dresses warmly, which nearly always involves leggings that mold to every fucking curve and my sweatshirt. I couldn't tell you which look I prefer more.

I bet she's not wearing a bra under my sweatshirt right now. I'm going to find out before I leave, I vow.

"Hey, sweetheart."

She jumps. "Don't sneak up on me, Max!"

I step the rest of the way into the room, bending at the waist so I can kiss her. I use one hand to gently tug her to her feet, still carefully holding the flowers in the other hand. "For you."

She takes them, blushing as predicted. "Max, you didn't have to."

"I never have to, but I always want to," I tell her, tilting her chin up so I can kiss her again. She's had more coffee, I think, that peppermint creamer obvious, and I lick into her mouth, chasing the flavor.

"What do you want for lunch?" she asks me when I pull back to let her breathe.

You is the first answer that comes to mind, and it's absolutely true and not appropriate, because I need to make sure she eats.

Now there's a thought. Sitting her at the table, plate in front of her, then sliding under the table and digging in.

I push it from my mind, though. Later. For now, I kiss her forehead. "You put the flowers in water, and I'll cook, alright?"

We have a panini press in the kitchen, because I'd discovered early on that Casey has a thing where she doesn't like cold sandwiches, and likes things all melted together. That had been easy to accommodate, even if she'd blushed and said the panini press was expensive and she could make a hot sandwich in a pan and I shouldn't worry about catering to her, anyway, and—

I'd stopped her spiral with a kiss that day, then made her a perfectly pressed panini, and I'll do the same today.

Two ham and cheese paninis later, paired with potato chips and the last of the grapes in our fridge and glasses of water, Casey is absently swinging her legs while sitting at the kitchen counter. Fucking adorable.

I want to stay in this moment forever, to not let who I am outside this house encroach on this moment, but I have no choice. "I can't come shopping with you," I tell her softly.

31

Her legs stop swinging. "Oh." It's like she's paralyzed for just a minute, but then forces a smile. I hate the forced smile, the way she covers up what she's feeling with so much practice. "That's okay. It was a long-shot; I know you have work."

"I do," I agree, reaching out to rub her thigh through her leggings. "But hey, listen. Work does not mean I'll neglect our home, alright? So, no more cleaning. I'll clean the rest of the house tonight." It feels shitty, because she clearly already did so much this morning, but I'll make it up to her. I will.

"You don't have to. It's my family coming over, I can—"

"You can accept that I'm going to support you," I interrupt, squeezing her thigh. "Baby, I know this is a lot."

She freezes, and I give up on the little squeezes to her thigh, instead hauling her into my lap, pulling her back against me, letting my thumbs stroke over her hips.

Everything feels better when I'm holding her like this. When all her warmth is right there, when her soft skin is in my hands. When I know nothing can happen to her because I am right here for her.

"They're my family," she whispers. "I should be able to..."

They're her family because she shares genetics with them, but I don't say that. I don't want to argue with her. She's convinced trying to reconcile with her family means progress, and I don't get to decide that it doesn't.

Was she born with an anxious brain, or did tip-toeing around her family and needing to be on high alert at every moment of every day to cater to their needs create the anxiety? We'll never know, I suppose, but either way, they didn't help her, and I am fully willing to blame them.

I'm not convinced her parents aren't narcissists, and the only child they ever loved was their golden child, their eldest son, who did all the things to reflect a shining light back on them.

Casey had the childhood Luc and I pretend I had on paper. Nice house, a dad with a respectable job, social climbers for parents. A good school and money for new clothes, especially when they'd be seen in public with them.

And if their daughter was shy? If she didn't know what to say, or didn't like prissy designer clothes, or didn't want strangers touching her, or preferred solitary activities that don't fill out the picture-perfect family greeting card? Then they couldn't forgive her for that.

I've never met them. I thought I could go my whole life without ever wanting to—if only because I knew my instinct to kill them would make Casey sad—but if she's inviting them over, then I'll deal with it however she needs me to. If she needs me to hold her hand and smile, I'll do it. If she needs me to lay down some hard truths for them, I'll happily oblige. If she needs me to bury some bodies, then I can do that too.

I squeeze her tighter. "No should, baby. We do this as a team, okay?"

Which just makes me feel like shit, because some team when I'm abandoning her this afternoon.

It's for us, I remind myself. It's for our future.

"Call me if you need anything when you're out, alright?" I say, pressing a kiss to the top of her head. "And I mean anything."

Will I be able to answer? Fuck it, that's non-negotiable. If she needs me, I'm picking up the damned phone.

This is for us, I remind myself. For us. And if all goes well, I can tell her soon.

December 23rd, 2:00 pm

The first whiff of that receipt is a painful blast to the past. Alexander. How many mornings had we lived in fear of that scent? How many times had we cringed when we smelled him coming?

And now I'm going towards it.

I'm not afraid of anything. I kill my enemies with ruthless efficiency. I've adapted to a hundred new times and places. I escaped the hell that was Alexander.

I remind myself that I have nothing in the world to fear. Then, when that doesn't work, I remind myself that I'm doing this for Casey and I.

Okay, that works. I stand a little taller. For Casey. I can do anything for Casey.

Fuck, I hope her shopping is going okay. I helped her make her list before I left, then did my best to be subtle when making sure she had the things that seem to help her the most—headphones to block out noise, a sweatshirt that goes down over her hands so people can't accidentally touch her bare skin, and a pack of gum because she can bite her nails when she gets anxious but has been trying hard to quit. That's not nearly enough, but it's the best I can do.

I know what she'd tell me if I brought that up. She'd say something totally self-deprecating that would make my blood boil, and then tell me that I can't do everything for her. And that's true. I know it is, but it doesn't stop me from wanting to make things easier for her.

She makes my life worth living, so it seems like the fairest trade-off. If I could, I would smooth out every bump in the world for her, take down every obstacle, and wrap her in bubble wrap. I'd do whatever I had to, kill whoever I needed to, pay whatever it cost, to make her life easier. And she'd kill me for doing it, I know. Or at the very least, she wouldn't forgive me, and I'd much rather her physically attack me than just leave me.

I can't make the world perfect for her. But I can make sure she has her headphones when she goes out.

So I resist pulling out my phone to call and check in, and focus on the job at hand.

The scent gets interrupted for long stretches, other scents obscuring Alexander's. Time erases everything, and cars are hell for tracking. Even so, I've been doing this for a while now, and I'm not worried.

Luc has never given me a target that I didn't eventually find.

The houses thin out, the plots of land keep growing bigger, and I keep going. I have to periodically pull over and stop the car, stepping out to get a better scent. Cars are nice for speed, and a convenient place to store a body when it needs to be moved, but they're a pain in the ass for scent tracking.

But I've caught the scent, and I'm positive that if he's not currently at the big old farmhouse set a half mile or so back from the road, then he's left recently enough that I could probably run him down.

I park before the bend in the road fully reveals the house, pulling my car off to the side, and make my way up to the door on foot.

What do you say to the man who made you when you see him for the first time in two thousand years? What do you say when you need something from him?

No, really, I don't mind the torture you put us through. The regular beatings and forcing us to fight to the death just made us stronger, no problem. Sorry about the escaping thing. Hey, can I know the secret for immortality, and will you come quietly back to my boss who definitely wants to put a stake through your heart? Somehow, I don't think that's going to quite cut it.

Fuck it. If Luc wanted pretty words, then he should have come himself. I bang on the door; subtlety was never my strongest suit.

A shotgun is leveled at my face when the door swings open, and I look down the barrel, entirely unimpressed. "That'll do jack shit," I tell him, looking past the weapon, disgusted to see a scared kid on the other end.

Oh, he holds firm. His hand on the gun doesn't shake, and his face doesn't waver. It's in his eyes, though. He's nervous about what might come next. I'd place him around seventeen or eighteen. He's a tall kid, but still gangly, like he hasn't grown into the size of his body yet. That, paired with the patchy attempt at facial hair, makes me think this is a genuine child in front of me.

"Put the gun down, kid," I tell him, keeping my feelings off my face. If he knows who I am—if Alexander told him that much—then he should be scared of me. "No one needs to get hurt if you let me in." Would I hurt this kid to get to Alexander?

For Casey? Without question.

"I…" He doesn't seem to have a complete thought to share, and he doesn't lower the gun. I think through the angles. I have a knife under my jacket, but drawing it will take too long, and I shouldn't need it. Not for one gangly kid, even if the kid has been trained by Alexander.

I don't want to kill him, but I will if he attacks. I think I could put him down without doing permanent damage, but that's always a risk in the heat of the moment, especially when you don't know what your opponent is capable of.

Fuck, what the hell does Alexander need immortal pet soldiers for these days? It's not like you can sneak a were-creature into the front lines and have it written off as the gods sending some sort of legendary warrior. Wolves don't just appear on the battlefield these days.

I raise an eyebrow. It doesn't really matter what Alexander trained him for, or how competent he is. He's seventeen, and my age is a multiple of his. I've been doing this for a long, long time. "Last chance, kid." I take a subtle sniff, scenting the house. Alexander is either here or he just left. Other than that, the scents of the house are stale, at least hours old if not entire days. "I'm not here for you. I'm here for Alexander."

At the sound of the name, the kid firms up his grip on the shotgun, and I worry for half a second that I really am going to get shot at point-blank range. It won't kill me, but it will be deeply unpleasant, and it might do enough damage that I won't be able to go home to Casey tonight.

Fuck it, that's not acceptable. I move faster than the kid could possibly hope to predict, knocking the gun to one side and then breaking his arm at the elbow, forcing him to drop it.

He screams, not disciplined enough to control it, and I wince. The sound is ear-splitting, and if I was a good man, I'd feel bad for hurting a kid. But all I can think is to be surprised that Alexander hadn't beaten the reaction out of him yet.

"Jacob. Let him in."

I don't lessen my grip on the kid, even as he goes nearly limp. I hold him upright, but turn my attention to the figure standing at the base of the staircase.

Alexander.

He looks the same. Perhaps he's not as tall as in my memory, and his eyes, while bright, don't quite have the air of hellfire I'd remembered, but overall it's the same man, unchanged through the ages.

He frowns at me. "You're one of mine."

I'm not his anything. I'm Luc's killer and I'm Casey's man and I'm my own monster, but I'll be damned before I am this man's anything ever again. I don't say anything, just shaking the kid slightly when he squirms, whimpering still about his arm.

Alexander looks him over dispassionately. "He's not full grown yet; that'll take weeks to heal." He says it so matter-of-factly, like he's reading a weather report. "It might be better to put him down."

The kid whimpers a little louder, but he doesn't protest or try to escape.

Fuck, I'm a killer, I try to remind myself. I've killed probably thousands. But I don't think I've ever killed an already-wounded kid, not when he was still perfectly savable.

I put him behind me and release my grip. He doesn't run, just lingering behind me, despite the way out being clear. The hairs on the back of my neck stand on end to have him at my vulnerable back, but I ignore him.

"You haven't changed," I say, the first words I've said to Alexander since the day Luc and I escaped.

It's like my voice gives him the last piece of the puzzle he needs to crack my identity. He smiles. "Maximus. You are one of mine. It's been a long time."

That name should be enough to strike fear into him. I've had people piss themselves when they hear I've come around. Luc has spent so many centuries using me to further his cause, to keep creatures in line, and to enforce his edicts, that I've become a ghost story in some circles. There should be fear in his eyes, a shiver down his spine.

Some fear would be gratifying. Something, anything, to tell me that this is different now, that this isn't like when I was a child. That I hold my own power here, and he's not going to debate putting me down like he did for Jacob.

"You've grown up," he states, completely calm.

I don't say anything back. I don't want to give him any more ammunition.

He continues, like my response is entirely unnecessary. "You were always the biggest of the litter, though, weren't you? And still the biggest, clearly. I named you appropriately. Tell me, are you here as Lucius' pet now?"

I want to bare my teeth at him.

I look around, even if I don't let my attention waver from him. He doesn't seem like much of a physical threat—he'd always needed a whip to discipline us to his standards back in the day, and I don't see a single weapon on him—but I won't underestimate this monster.

"A bit of a come-down from your own private fighting pits in the emperor's home, yeah?" I ask, studying what was clearly a homey farmhouse. It's run-down now, but someone left a stenciled live, laugh, love on one wall, and a home is where the heart is over the kitchen doorway.

"You should see the basement," he says.

I think I would rather eat glass.

"It's been millennia," he continues. "Don't tell me your runt cut you loose? Looking for a new master?"

I'm not anyone's fucking pet, I want to say, but I bite my tongue. I've never had to work so hard not to make my feelings known in my life. Usually, when someone pisses me off, I can let my fists do the talking. Unfortunately, that's not going to cut it today.

"Are you inviting me in, or do I need to kill him?" I say, jerking my thumb over my shoulder without turning my attention to Jacob.

Alexander shrugs. "You'd be saving me the trouble. I don't have time to coddle animals that can't take care of themselves." My blood feels hot, like my rage could cause me to just boil over.

I shouldn't be surprised. I shouldn't be capable of being surprised, not when this is exactly the same as it was when I was a child. We were useful, or we were beaten. And if it was especially bad, we were killed. We fought each other, and no one shed tears if one day someone didn't walk away.

I've tried so hard not to think about that. That was the time in my life when I'd been weakest; I'd been entirely at Alexander's mercy. It didn't matter if the other boys couldn't kill me, if I always walked away from fights. I was just as vulnerable to him as any of us.

It's painful to remember, and I haven't wanted to. So I've avoided it, especially recently. What do I need my past for? I have a future I want desperately.

But here Alexander is, doing the same shit to a new generation of monster kids. I spare half a glance behind me towards Jacob. "You can run," I tell him. "I won't fucking stop you."

He goes painfully still. "My place is here," he says, his voice barely a whisper.

Alexander chuckles. "We've worked on loyalty since your day, Maximus. Now, come in. Tell me what you and that little upstart that holds your leash are looking for."

December 23rd, 3:30 pm

There's a layer of dust on the table. I'm not surprised that no one eats here; we always ate like animals, food thrown on the floor for us whether we were in human or animal form, and I doubt Alexander has changed that particular practice.

Alexander sits at the head of the table like he's a king sitting in a banquet hall. He snaps his fingers, and the kid comes hurrying forward, turning into a sleek panther as he gets near, then laying next to the chair. His eyes and ears remain alert, but I can see his paw held at an unnatural angle.

"You usually have a whole litter, from what I hear," I say, letting my eyes pass over the kid before focusing entirely on Alexander.

"Jacob here was a little too housebroken. Good for menial tasks, and I needed an assistant. Less desirable to my buyers. So I'm left with him. Well, I was—we'll see if he lasts the day." The threat is said so casually, and none of us react to it at all. Not even the boy whose life he's threatening, although

I know damned well that he can hear just fine in his panther form.

"A bit like your master, honestly. Or at least, as we all assumed—housebroken. Not made for war."

Lucius is small, and he isn't ever going to win battles on strength alone. But he's smarter than all of us combined, and twice as lethal, and that's always been how he survived. It's how we escaped, and it's how I'm here now.

"So, tell me—what does that runt want from me?"

"Who says I'm here for him?"

He raises a mocking eyebrow. "Because I know you, Maximus. You couldn't wipe your own ass without someone giving you the order. You like taking orders. A much more comfortable place for you. If it isn't mine anymore, then it's Lucius'. No shame in that—it means the training worked. You, at least, bred true." He nudges the panther on the floor with his foot. "I hate to waste good product."

My throat is suddenly dry. "I'm not yours," is all I can say.

"You could be. If that's why you're here, then we can talk."

I'd rather chew my own arm off.

"I've kept tabs on you," he continues. "You and Lucius, and all my other cast-offs you've scrounged up."

"Lucius kept tabs on you too."

"I know," he says darkly. "The runt is a pain in the ass. I should have had someone kill him eons ago."

"You would have had to go through me."

"Oh, I'm aware. And you've made a name for yourself, haven't you?" I don't answer; we both know that I have. "Is this the life you wanted? Is this different from what I promised you?"

"At least I'm the one in control now," I say.

"Are you? Or is that Lucius?"

It is absolutely Lucius, and that's the galling thing. I promised my life away to him if he got me away from Alexander, and so far I haven't strayed. I fulfilled my bargain, but I immediately sold my life away again.

But that was for Casey. Just thinking about her reminds me why I'm here.

I debate my options. Seeing him threaten to put the boy down threw me, I admit it. I never should have sat at a table with him. Who the fuck do I think I am? I've never solved a problem with words in my life.

"I run my life, Alexander," I tell him, turning over options in my mind. "And your time is up."

"Oh, is it?" He has the audacity to chuckle when he speaks, the most emotion he's shown the entire time I've been here. "You and what army?"

I glance down at the panther. "I don't think he can stop me."

"You've forgotten about me already? Maybe I need to remind you of the damage I can do."

The panther whines, something that, in my day, would have been greatly punished. Maybe the training is slipping if that reaction wasn't trained out of Jacob long ago. "Big talk. I think if you had that type of magic, you'd have used it. But you need a whip to be tough, don't you? And I don't see one. Forget it in the basement?"

His lip curls. "Your master's insolence has rubbed off on you, hm?"

"I could drag you back to Lucius, torture you like he wants, and still get exactly what I want out of you," I tell him. I'm probably going to need to do that anyway—it's not like I can let Alexander continue to roam the world. Not now that we have incontrovertible proof that he's still turning kids into monsters.

"And if I wanted to avoid that messiness?" he asks. "Has your master authorized you to strike a deal?"

He hasn't, but then again, Lucius trusts me and my methods. A little catch and release never hurt anybody. I'll track him back down later.

"We're looking to know what you know. How to make beings immortal."

"Ah, is Lucius dissatisfied with his current roster of pets? Looking to make his own?"

"Does it work on adults?" I ask, firmly ignoring his question. "Or does it only work on infants?"

"Infants are easier," he says. "Get them that young, you can really rear up the animal in them. It's always easier to train them when they're young. Before they learn too many human habits. Think they're worth something."

"But it's possible," I press. "You can do it to an adult?"

"Why does Lucius want to know?" He squints for a moment, studying me, then smiles, a slow unfolding that makes my hair stand on end. "You want to know. You're not here for Lucius after all, are you? Did the beast fall in love with some fragile little mortal beauty?"

That hits a little too close to home. I don't want Casey's name in his mouth. I don't want her existence to even cross his mind. I want to keep her so very far from this world.

Before I can figure out what to say, the panther at my feet makes a yapping sound. The pain must be getting to him, so I ignore it—there's really nothing I can do for him. But then he makes the sound again.

I dart a quick glance downward, and his eyes are wide, staring directly at me. I take a deep draw of air. Fuck. There's another scent approaching this place. Alexander had been keeping me distracted.

Alexander realizes Jacob is communicating at the same time I do, and he curses and kicks the panther. "We're leaving now," he snaps at him. "Come or die."

"I don't think so." I push to my feet.

Alexander's cold smirk returns. "I wouldn't do that, Maximus. You'll never learn how to save your fragile little mortal if you fight me."

I doubt he's going to just tell me if I don't, but I don't waste time with words. Alexander was right about one thing; bargaining has never really been my strong suit.

Ignoring Jacob, I lunge for Alexander, hoping to neutralize him before whatever new threat arrives.

"Impertinent child," he snaps, and drops a handful of something onto the table. The room erupts into flames.

The breath is entirely knocked out of me when I hit the ground, and I'm forced to close my eyes against the brightness of the flames. When the brightness behind my lids fades, I hesitantly open my eyes, trying to take stock of the damage.

I don't think I'm burned. Either the fire was just some sort of illusion, or it wasn't hot enough to do any actual damage to a creature like me. I spring to my feet, only to get bowled over again.

Another fucking panther, and this one isn't Jacob.

I can also tell that this one isn't a damned kid. There's no juvenile ranginess left in the frame; a solid wall of muscle knocks me back.

Fuck this. I grit my teeth and let the wolf in me take control, turning the fight into one that's animal to animal. It's not much of a fight, but then it never is anymore. I clamp my mouth around his neck and rip his throat out between my teeth. He yips, and then he can't make sound anymore. He shudders in the grip of my jaw, and then goes still.

I release him, spitting the blood out of my mouth. The animal doesn't particularly care, but I've learned from experience that the human definitely minds.

Of course, I've also learned from experience that I can hold onto the blood and let it drip from my mouth to make a point if I need to. Unfortunately, Alexander and Jacob are already gone, so there's no one to make a point to. I force myself up onto four legs, trying to get their scent, but all I can smell is blood and fire. Growling, I smash my way through a window, letting the broken glass cut me, not caring in the slightest as I push for fresh air, trying to catch the scent.

All I can smell is the gas fumes of a fucking car. I try to chase after it, but on these wide open roads, a car can outpace a wolf. And they already had a head start on me.

I push myself faster and faster, trying to catch up to the car, keeping my nose to the ground to follow the scent. But then their car's scent mingles with others, and a wolf can't run alongside a busy road without drawing the wrong sort of attention.

I howl my frustration before forcing the human version of myself to take control once more. Fuck. This.

I lost my one chance to give Casey the life we both deserve. And Alexander is still out there, doing who knows what terrible things to whoever he still has in his power.

I look up at the sun, already setting. Fuck it. I'm not going to get anywhere else today, but this isn't over. I've never lost a target before, and I won't start today. Alexander's time is limited, and I just need a moment to formulate a plan.

I look down at myself. My clothes are in tatters, which isn't unexpected from turning. That's fine, and I have a change in my car. The bigger problem is the blood and cuts.

The cuts don't look deep, so they'll be healed before I get home. But I can't go back with blood all over my skin. I'll need to find a stream to clean up in before I can go back amongst human company.

But first, I need to get to my car. I have a lighter in the glove box, and I'm thinking that the farmhouse could use some redecorating.

December 23rd, 8:00 pm

I t takes longer than I thought it would. I have to watch the entire house burn, keeping a careful eye on it so it doesn't burn the surrounding woods. Then, on my way to find a stream, I decide to follow the scent of the dead shifter who attacked me, trying to determine where he'd been.

He's been all over these woods, so I walk in circles for a bit, nose to the ground, but eventually I find where the scent is strongest.

It's some sort of training pit, not entirely dissimilar to the ones I was raised in. There are targets and training dummies, weapons stacked with military precision, an obstacle course, and cages on one side. I can smell the blood that seeps into the soil, and I know without having to check that more than one kid died here and was buried here.

Fucking hell.

I've ignored Alexander for millennia. I knew, logically, he was still out there; Luc kept bringing back strays like us, and each of them had come with a similar story of how Alexander bred and raised them to kill. But I'd never crossed paths with him. I'd never gone looking. I'd considered myself lucky to have escaped with my life all those years ago and focused on my work, and that had been the end of it.

After a dip in a stream and some vigorous scrubbing to get rid of the blood, I make my way back to my car, pull on clean clothes, and start the drive home.

When I open the front door, I'm relieved to find that the scent of cleaning products isn't stronger than it was this morning. The house must be basically spotless, because I know Casey and I know she did a good job earlier, but at least she took my advice and left whatever's left for me to do.

I'm less relieved to realize that the house is dark, and I don't hear her moving around.

"Sweetheart? I'm home," I say, toeing off my shoes and moving through the house, looking over the kitchen and living room as I pass, then going upstairs to our bedroom and the offices. Her office is dark, and I don't know if that's a good or a bad sign. I don't want her working, but lying in bed at eight in the evening isn't great, either.

"Sweetheart?" I ask softly, pushing our bedroom door open.

She's lying on top of the covers, like she flopped there and gave up. I speed-walk over to her, sitting on the blanket beside her, and stroke her hair away from her face. "What's going on, baby?"

"Nothing," she murmurs, face half in the pillow. "I'm just tired."

Yeah, no shit. Even her voice sounds like the energy has been entirely drained out of her. I hate lying in bed fully clothed, but I ignore that and lie down so I can scoop her into my arms, squeezing her to me.

She immediately wiggles a bit to somehow get impossibly closer.

It's like my own exhaustion, my own worry, my own problems drain out of me as soon as I have her in my arms. She says I'm like a heated, weighted blanket, and she is the softest, best-smelling pillow I've ever held.

I run my nose through her dark hair, finding that spot behind her ear. "Want to talk, sweetheart?" The answer is probably no, but I wait patiently anyway. I want her to know I'm here, that I'm always here, even on days like today when I basically abandoned her.

"Groceries are put away," she mumbles. "I got everything on the list."

Good job sounds patronizing, so I don't say it. I just kiss her ear.

"Do you have to work tomorrow?" she asks me, voice even softer.

My heart falls like a rock. Fuck, I hate myself and my job and Luc and the whole damned world I'm hiding from her at this moment. "Yeah, baby. Only part of the day though."

I need to sort this out. I need to make some sort of progress before I lose Alexander's trail entirely. And not just for Casey and I, although that is a big part of it. But I can't let him go on doing what he has been doing. I can't let him get away with what he did to us.

But also for Casey and I. I'm not going to lose this chance at a future for us.

She nods. "I took the whole day, so I'll finish cleaning. Would you…" She trails off, her universal sign that she actually needs something from me but is afraid to ask and inconvenience me.

Fuck that. I'm desperate to be inconvenienced by her, and fuck anyone who ever made her feel otherwise.

"Would I what?" I prompt, running my hand up and down her spine. "'Cause you already know the answer is yes, sweetheart."

"The restaurant said the ham would be ready at three. Could you pick it up on your way home?" she asks, and it sounds like she's asking me to donate a kidney with the level of gravity she asks it with.

I'd absolutely donate a kidney to her. I'll drive to a restaurant too. "Yeah, sweetheart. I'll do that. What else?"

She shakes her head. "That's it. Everything else I got today." We'd agreed to order the ham from a restaurant, since neither of us have any clue how to prepare it well. She said we could handle the rest of it. I'm a shit cook all the way around, but I'll do whatever she asks. Besides, if her parents don't like our cooking, then they can just not come over.

"I'll just cook it tomorrow, after I finish cleaning." I don't want her to spend tomorrow cooking and cleaning. I fucking hate the idea, actually. I might not be able to help with the cooking if I'm going to be chasing down Alexander, but I sure as shit can handle the cleaning situation.

"Nope," I say, kissing her temple and forcing myself to sit up. She whines slightly as I let her go, which tugs at my heartstrings, but I keep moving. "Don't move for a minute, sweetheart."

I run to the bathroom and start the bath, plugging the drain when it's just this side of boiling. Casey likes to make human soup out of herself, but I'm definitely not going to argue about it today.

I drop in a bath bomb. It's one of the lavender ones Casey likes, and it's the last one. Well, the last one until Christmas, at least, because there are three in my office closet, just waiting to get stuffed into her stocking.

"Okay, baby," I say, walking back into our bedroom. "Let's get you in the bath."

She perks her head up. "You going to join me?"

Don't I wish. But she'll thank me more tomorrow if I take care of the basic things that need to be addressed before I think about being all wet and naked with her.

Nothing says I can't multitask, though. If I get the chores done fast enough, I can join her in the bath. Hold her, all wet and slick and soapy. Maybe slip my fingers inside her and make her fall apart for me. There's no better incentive that I can think of.

"I'm going to go get the cleaning done," I tell her. "All of it. And then I'll bring you up something to eat, because I know you and I highly doubt you had anything after you got home." Her silence speaks louder than any response could. "And then I'll join you, okay, sweetheart?"

"You don't have to do the cleaning. It's my family."

"Nope," I tell her, trying to keep my voice firm but also cheerful. "My house too, baby. Now, can I help you to the bath?"

She lets me help her up and tug off her clothes, leaving the leggings and overly large sweatshirt in a pile on the floor for us to worry about later. Then I get her settled in the bath. "Want some music?"

She nods, so I fiddle with the speaker for a minute, turning on something soft and soothing. Then, with one last look at her in the bath, head tilted back and eyes closed, I slip out the door.

Right, a clean house. I put one headphone in, leaving the other ear free to listen for anything Casey might need. Then, I turn on music with a little more punch. I'm not looking to relax, after all; I'm looking to get some work done fast.

She vacuumed earlier, so I mop the kitchen, scrub the downstairs bathroom, and change out the tablecloth to something a little more decorative. I take a moment to set the table with the nicest dishes we own—admittedly, they're not especially nice—so she doesn't have to think about that when she's cooking tomorrow.

I straighten the shelves in the living room, taking a minute to put the most intellectual-looking books on top of the others, and double-check that we caught any stray crumbs that might have fallen into the couch cushions. Casey's hair is so fucking beautiful, but it can shed like crazy, so I run a keen eye over the place, looking for loose curls on the furniture or floors, just in case.

There. Assuming we don't allow guests upstairs, then we should be fine.

I make sure all the cleaning supplies are entirely put away, then take an extra long minute to listen for Casey. There's a slight splashing sound, and her soothing music, but that's it.

That gives me enough time to put together a small plate, toasting a plain bagel and spreading peanut butter on it, then slicing a banana to add on top. A perfect Casey is having a bad day meal. I add a glass of water, absolutely sure she didn't drink enough today, and go back upstairs.

I should get her one of those trays you put over a bathtub. I wonder if it's too late to get it shipped here before Christmas. Probably, but that's okay, because it'll make a perfect "just because" gift in the next few weeks. In the meantime, I set the food on the counter, there for when I get her out of the bath.

"Ready to get out?" I ask, holding up the biggest, fluffiest towel we own.

She turns to face me, opening her eyes and her arms, smiling softly. "Food can wait."

"You need to eat."

"I will. But, join me? You've had a long day too."

She's so fucking good to me. She doesn't know the half of it, and thankfully all my injuries from earlier have disappeared, but she still sees straight through me, and wants to make sure I'm taken care of too.

"Okay, baby. Give me a minute." I pull my clothes off and drop them in a pile with hers, a problem for later. Then I reach in and pull the bath drain, letting a little of the water go before re-plugging it and filling it with more hot water. "Budge up, sweetheart. Give me some room." She scoots forward, and I slide in behind her, sitting her between my legs.

I don't usually like my bath water as hot as Casey does, but I have to admit that it feels good on my overworked muscles. I groan, then pull her back into me, and suddenly it feels even better. The world narrows down to just her and me, and everything else fades away.

Unfortunately, Casey clearly isn't on the same page yet. That's fine, and expected—her brain will keep on turning over the stuff happening outside this bathroom forever if we don't redirect it. "What're you thinking about?"

"What's left to do tomorrow? So I can make a list so I can start planning a schedule and make sure I'm on time for everything and—"

I squeeze her waist. "Nothing's left, baby. Nothing. You don't worry about any of the cleaning tomorrow, okay?" I pick up her hand so I can kiss her now-pruney fingers. Her tattoos end at the wrist, one sleeve of flowers, the other of celestial bodies. Her hands are completely clear of any ink, and I kiss over them, wondering for the thousandth time if she'd like tattooed wedding bands. I bet she would.

Fuck, that would do something to me. Tattoo or metal—or both—on her hand, where I could see it whenever I looked over, would completely ruin my life. I'd never do anything productive ever again.

What a perfect fucking future. And one that might be entirely in my grasp, if I can just find Alexander tomorrow.

And there I go, thinking about things outside this room instead of what I have right here, right now. It seems that Casey and I both need something to refocus us.

I suck two of her fingers into my mouth, teasing at them for a second before I kiss her palm and then lower her hand. "I want to make you feel good, baby. Help you relax. Can I do that? Please?"

I'm pleading and I couldn't give less of a fuck. I've never pleaded in my life before I met this woman. I didn't plead for my life in battle, I didn't plead for torture to stop. But with Casey? I'll beg all damned day long.

"Please," she whispers, like she's the one asking me for a favor. Goddamn, I'm going to make her come until she forgets her own name. I'm going to make her mind be so consumed with pleasure that there simply won't be room left for the anxiety.

I pinch her left nipple, lightly at first, then firming up my grip when she groans. When she squirms lightly, I release her nipple, studying the reddened, slightly swollen bud, before I move onto the right for equality's sake.

Can't have one tit thinking I like it better than the other. Not when they're both some of the most beautiful things I've ever seen.

I trail the hand that's been on her waist up higher, tracing feather-light fingers along the under-boob tattoo, a beautiful array of flowers. She always moans so prettily when I touch her there, and today is no exception.

I release my hold on her nipple, and she pushes her tits forward, subconsciously seeking more. "Pretty girl," I croon, bending closer so I can whisper directly in her ear. "So fucking pretty for me, hm?" She shivers again.

Never has there been a more perfect marriage, because all I want in life is to say these things all day long, and all she needs is to hear them.

"I'm going to make you come, sweetheart," I tell her. "You just lay back and relax, okay? Let me make you feel good." She nods, a lethargic, slow movement that she finishes by tipping her head back onto my chest, trying to look up at me, and, well, I have to reward that, don't I?

The angle for the kiss is terrible, but I couldn't give less of a fuck, determined to have her lips on mine, to taste her sweet mouth, to have every damned inch of her. When she tilts her head even further to deepen the kiss, I slide my hand down from her tits to her cunt, teasing right along the seam.

She groans into the kiss and tries to spread her legs, slightly inhibited by the size of the tub and my legs surrounding hers. Can't have that—I need her to be nice and open for me, ready to take all the damned pleasure that I can give her.

It takes a minute of maneuvering, but at last I hook her legs over mine, using them to keep her spread wide for me. "Such a pretty girl," I croon, looking over her shoulder and down her body. I don't have the best view of her cunt from here, but I can feel it, wet and slick and open against my teasing fingers, and that's enough to make my hard cock press into her back. I can't help it, grinding against her for a second before I grab back at my control.

Casey first. And, if I have my way, second and third. Then, I can think about coming, and hopefully inside her hot, tight cunt.

I circle her clit slowly, gently, like I have all the time in the world. She suppresses her moan, and that just won't do. I need to draw those out of her for my sanity. I need to hear her falling apart for me. I up the pressure just slightly on my next pass, and I hear the tiniest catch of breath. I bury my face in her hair, hiding my smile against her scalp. There we go.

"C'mon, Casey," I murmur. "You're so fucking good, baby. Let yourself go. Let yourself feel this."

I dip closer to her entrance to gather more of her wetness, slick and hot, and then bring it back up to circle her clit.

When I think of heaven, this right here is what I dream of. Her hair smells so damned good, her body is soft and pliant in my arms, her hips are making small little movements, hungry for more, and her breathing is getting more desperate. I could live in this moment forever.

And then she actually moans. "Max," she gasps, and that's my cue. She's let go of the day, she's here now, and she's ready for me to bring this to the next level.

Without any warning, I push two fingers inside her cunt, reveling in the aborted little shout, cut off by a moan that sounds like it comes all the way from her toes.

This isn't my favorite position to have her in, because the angles can leave a lot to be desired. But I'll make do, crooking my fingers to find her g-spot and using my thumb to brush her clit.

She screams, and then her mouth falls open without a single sound emerging. She goes boneless, completely trusting her pleasure to me, knowing I'll get her where she needs to go. Fuck, that's a heady feeling. And an honor, too, knowing I've proven myself to her, that she just knows I'll get her there, that she trusts me with something so precious as her body. As her pleasure.

"Come for me, baby," I murmur to her, making sure I brush her g-spot. Her legs tense over mine, trying and failing to close so she can trap my hand where she wants it. Like I would ever remove my fingers when she's so damn close. Like I would ever deny myself the sight of her coming apart.

"C'mon, sweetheart, pretty girl," I continue, knowing she's listening, knowing she needs to hear it almost as much as I need to say it. "C'mon, my perfect fucking woman, you're doing so good for me, so fucking beautiful like this. Let me make you come, sweetheart. Let your man give you what you need."

I'm hard as steel against her back, but I ignore my cock, determined to get her there, to feel her fall apart for the first time tonight before I think of anything else.

She's so fucking perfect like this, letting me give her what she needs. It fucking rips me open, makes me feel things I didn't even know that I was capable of. Like my heart was just a dead organ in my chest until she brought it to life. Like she's the very reason I breathe.

"Come for me, baby," I murmur, feeling how close she is, how desperate. I stroke her g-spot, thumbing her clit at the same time, and she gives me what we both need, shattering in my hold, panting my name like the word is forced out of her.

"Good girl," I tell her. I'm not sure she can really hear me right now, but if she can, she's damn well going to hear me reassuring her. "Fucking beautiful, perfect girl. I love you so goddamn much."

And as I talk, I continue to stroke her, letting her cunt squeeze my fingers over and over, convulsing as I push her towards another orgasm.

The best way to get Casey out of her head? Fuck her until her whole body is entirely subsumed by pleasure. Overstimulate her senses in a completely different way.

She thrashes a little, but she can't move her legs when I'm holding her like this. All she can do is give into pleasure or tell me to stop, and, judging by the way she's moaning "Max," over and over, I doubt stop is currently on her mind.

"Going to come for me again, sweetheart?" I ask her, using my free hand to spread across her belly, holding her to me and stroking the soft flesh there. "Going to make my day and let me see that?"

Her head shakes in a way that might be a nod, or might just be her losing control of her body. I honestly can't tell, but it doesn't really matter, because the result is the same.

"Feel what you do to me, beautiful?" I ask her, giving in to the temptation to grind against her back for just a moment. "Because you are so fucking perfect, Casey. You're the best damn thing I've ever seen, and touching you is a fucking honor. Making you come is what dreams are made of, baby. Can you come again for me, sweetheart?"

She's beyond words, only able to say my name in a desperate little plea that makes me feel thirty feet tall. God, I fucking love this girl and every little thing she does.

I can feel her getting closer, her cunt fluttering around my fingers, like it's surrendering to whatever pleasure I want to give it. "Come for me, sweetheart," I murmur, and she does.

Her second orgasms always make me think of storms, violent and sudden and seemingly taking over her whole body. They leave her exhausted afterwards, too, but in a satiated, well-fucked sort of way.

I use my hand on her stomach to cradle her to me, and my fingers in her cunt to give her something to squeeze around. She milks them like they're my cock, her body jerking as the pleasure wrecks her.

"Perfect fucking woman," I tell her softly when I think she can hear me again. Her legs shake even as the rest of her has gone boneless, wrung out and showing me that this was a job well done. "You're so goddamned beautiful when you come for me, Casey. I'm the luckiest man alive."

I'd do fucking anything to keep having these moments forever, I think, then squash the thought because that defeats the purpose of this. We're not thinking of anything beyond the here and now. Nothing about tomorrow exists, not yet. Right now, it's just her, and me, and this perfect moment.

She's pliant and soft in my arms, not talking, just breathing as I stroke her, this time stroking her outer thighs, her hips, her stomach, her ribs, her arms, more focused on soothing her than arousing her.

Casey's body is usually tense enough that I worry she'll shatter. I've seen soldiers more relaxed before battle. It's like the anxiety locks all her muscles up even when she doesn't express being especially anxious about anything. And the only time I can change that and get her to relax completely is moments like this.

If she falls asleep in my arms, then that's no problem for me. I can dry her off and carry her to bed just fine. She used to worry that she would be too much for me to carry, but I've firmly proven her wrong a thousand times by now.

She doesn't fall asleep, though. When the water is getting cold, she stirs and tries to reach behind her for my cock. "You didn't come."

"Not yet," I agree, leaning down to kiss at her neck. "I'm not worried about it, baby." I'm still hard as diamonds behind her, but that can wait. If she's sleepy, I can jerk off once she's out for the night. I just held her as she came in my arms twice, watching her tits bounce and hearing her moan my name like it's a lifeline—it's not like I don't have plenty of jerk-off material.

She squirms, clearly more concerned with it than I am. "Do you want to fuck me?"

I pause, considering. I'd worry about her being over-sensitive, about me having pushed her cunt too far already, but if she's offering, then she wants it. Her offering because she feels like she has to is something we worked through long ago, and she knows better than to offer when she's not up for it now.

But if I fuck her like I want to, we'll make a huge mess in here. The entire bathroom will be soaked in the overflowing water. We've already made a little mess around the tub, heedless of sloshing water as I got her off.

That's alright. I won't let her focus on it, and I'll clean it up after she falls asleep.

"You know the answer to that," I tell her. "I always want to fuck you. In bed, though, okay?"

I'm still holding her legs in place with my own, so I relax enough that she can stand. I stand behind her, eyeing her naked, wet form hungrily. Then I step out, grabbing a towel before moving to help her out. I dry her gently before wrapping her in the towel and grabbing one of my own.

She takes a second towel and squeezes out the ends of her curls, which got a little damp from our escapades. "Do you need to do anything about these?" I ask, gently tugging the end of one and watching it spring back.

"I'll take care of it tomorrow, when I'm getting ready," she says, and I have a moment to think about her getting ready. Is she planning to dress up for tomorrow? I take half a second to be resentful of her putting in effort for assholes who probably won't properly appreciate it.

Screw them. I'll appreciate the hell out of it.

I kiss her temple. "Okay, baby. Why don't you go get comfortable for me in bed, hm?"

"How do you want me?"

"However you want, Casey. Make sure you're comfortable." I've already made her come twice tonight and worn her out to the point where I genuinely thought she'd fall asleep on me a few minutes ago. I'm not going to ask for any acrobatics.

"Got it," she says, and then deliberately puts the towel I'd wrapped around her back on the rack, walking into our bedroom completely naked, giving me a spectacular view of her ass.

God damn. I fight back a groan, completely losing my train of thought as I watch her leave.

When she's through the door, I force myself to focus, toweling myself dry and then throwing my towel onto the floor, pushing it around with one foot to soak up as much of the water we spilled as possible. Then I turn off the speaker, cutting off the calming strains of music that I didn't even notice under her delicious moans.

There, that'll have to be good enough. I can hear the bed frame moving as she gets comfortable, and I'd have to be a way stronger man to resist her a moment longer.

When I get into the bedroom, she's lying down on her back, hands up by her head, and I know what that means. She needs me to hold her down a little, to surround her and give her exactly what she needs without letting her overthink it.

Perfect.

"So fucking beautiful," I tell her, looking over her entire body, letting my eyes linger. "Be a good girl and put those hands under the pillow."

She does as I ask, and she doesn't pout or anything, but I can see the slight frown. She doesn't want to restrain herself; she wants me to do it for her.

And I will. But I hope she'll forgive me for the slight deviation in her plan.

I haven't tasted her cunt since six thirty this morning. I couldn't even lick my fingers properly clean during our bath. And that needs to be rectified immediately.

I'm on her before she even finishes sliding her hands under the pillow, hands on her hips to pull her to my mouth. I tug her further down the bed towards me, which probably rips the pillow out of her grip, but I couldn't fucking care less.

I have her cunt in my mouth, and I'm content to stay here until I die.

There are two ways to eat a woman out. One is what I did to her this morning, slow and teasing, working her up gently, guiding her to her orgasm. The other is pure desperation, eating cunt like it's my last meal, like I'm starving and will die if I don't have her, and that's more where I am right this minute.

She'll get pleasure. Her orgasm is inevitable at this point, and I won't rest until she comes. But I can't deny that when I eat her out this way, it's more for my pleasure than for hers.

She gasps and moans my name when I first start, clearly not expecting this. I push her legs wider, then gently grasp her ankles to keep them pushed back, giving me an unobstructed space to work with.

I'm settling in for a long haul, planning to be on my knees between her thighs until she finally calls it quits on me, but she has other ideas. She reaches down and grabs my hair, pulling me off of her, and I reluctantly move, face dripping as I look up at her.

She looks wrecked, absolutely on the edge again, and I know instinctively I could taste her orgasm with another minute or so of work. I want it, almost dip my head towards her cunt again, but her grip on my hair hasn't relaxed, and I don't dare move until she directs me.

"I want to come with you inside me," she says firmly.

Fuck, I love when she asks for things. I love it even better when she just takes them, but that almost never happens.

Still, my woman gets whatever the fuck she asks for, so I nod the best I can with her holding me by the hair. "Alright, baby. I'll fuck you so good. How do you want it? Soft so I can fuck you off to sleep? Harder?"

She smiles, a wicked edge to it that makes my cock leak and balls tighten. "Make me feel it tomorrow, Max."

I move up her body, dragging her thighs around my hips before I slide my hands over her wrists, pinning them to the bed. I'm careful about how much pressure I put on them, even though she always reminds me she's not breakable. And that's definitely true, because my Casey is made of iron. But I can break steel rods in half with one bare hand without even thinking about it, so I'll be extra careful about her precious bones.

With one hand wrapped around both wrists, I fist my cock, pumping twice before slotting myself at her entrance. "Tell me to stop if it's too much," I remind her.

She tightens her thighs on my hips. "Fuck me, Max."

Anything she asks for. I push all the way into her in one deep thrust, her cunt welcoming me inside immediately. I have to close my eyes against it, her wet heat absolutely exquisite.

She clenches down around me, like she's somehow worried I'd ever consider pulling out. "So fucking perfect, sweetheart," I grunt, pulling out so I can drive into her again. And again.

"Max," she whines, and that lights a fire inside me, my cock desperate for release. Fucking hell, my Casey is goddamn perfect, so tight around me, arching her body close with the limited mobility I've left for her, biting her lip to refrain from getting too loud.

I squeeze lightly at her wrists. "Don't bite that lip, baby. Let me hear you. Just us here."

Her moans are music to my ears and push me closer to the edge.

But I won't go over without her. Shifting to support myself on my knees, I find her clit with my free hand, stroking a few times before I trail my fingers down to where we're connected.

Fuck that, that's too fucking hot. I literally won't last.

"You getting close, baby?" I ask her, stroking over her clit again. I know she is, can feel it in every twitch, every squeeze, every breath. I know her body better than my own at this point. I've charted her every reaction like sailors charted the night skies, and I can find every single constellation of her. But I like hearing her voice, so I'm going to make her say it.

"Close," she gasps. A third orgasm in such a short period is pushing it for her, but she's grinding against me, seemingly hungry for it, and who the fuck am I to stop her?

"Then come for me, sweetheart," I say to her, voice low with hunger. "Come for me, Casey, squeeze my cock and push me over the edge. You're so goddamned beautiful when you come, give it to me, please—"

I'm pleading again and couldn't care less. Fuck it, I need her to come. Need to feel her squeezing around me, feel her claiming my cock, using it to make herself feel good—

Her mouth falls open into that perfect o, her legs and cunt clamping down on me as she spasms around me, her orgasm sweeping through her in a beautiful, perfect rush.

And that's all it takes to send me over the edge. My cock, desperate for her tonight, shoots jets of come inside her, my hips pumping frantically as she absolutely destroys me.

When I have sense again, I roll onto my back, pulling her so she's on top of me. I take her wrists in my hand, this time to bring them to my lips so I can kiss them gently. While I have them, I take a minute to look them over, making sure I never squeezed too tight.

She hums softly, contentedly, and I smile. That's my perfect girl. All relaxed and soft now, and only I can do that for her.

I stroke down her spine after I release her wrists. "You sleepy, sweetheart?"

She nods against my chest.

I move my hand to her hair, scratching lightly at her scalp. "Then you should sleep." This time, she shakes her head. "No? What's the matter?"

"I never asked you about your day," she says, her voice definitely exhausted but also determined.

I kiss the top of her head. "Well, I'm here with you. So my day is perfect, Casey. Could not ask for anything else."

"Something is going on at work," she insists, and now she sounds worried. For me. She's worried for me, because she's fucking perfect. My heart gets all tender and soft, and I somehow want to pull her closer, even though she's already on top of me.

"It won't be a big deal," I promise her, thinking about how I can phrase this to her. I hope I can tell her the whole story soon, but not until I have a way forward for us. "Just an old enemy of Luc's making trouble for us. But I swear, baby, I will be here for our party tomorrow. And I'll definitely be here for Christmas." I'll burn the entire world to the ground before I miss either day with her. Fuck everyone else.

"Can I help you?" she asks. Her eyes are drifting closed, her exhausting trip to the store earlier and all the work she did today and three orgasms catching up to her.

"You just did, sweetheart. So, thank you."

"You made me come three times," she protests.

"Incredibly rejuvenating stuff. Exactly what I need after a hard day." I'm dead serious when I say it. She might never understand just how serious I am about that, but I need her to at least get the gist.

She's it for me, and her presence is like the sun coming up in my life. I wouldn't survive without her.

"Promise?" she asks, and I think I hear a bit of that old insecurity creeping in.

It makes my heart hurt a bit, because I thought we'd worked through this, that she was fully aware that she's the light of my entire life. But there's a lot going on, a lot making her anxious. I'll just have to keep reminding her.

I give her a gentle squeeze. "I promise, baby. Casey, you are my entire damn world. None of it would be worth it without you."

She hums like she's agreeing, and then, between one breath and the next, she's asleep.

Good. She needs to sleep.

I wait until I'm sure she's deeply asleep before getting up to clean the rest of the bathroom, then silently poking around the house, seeing if there's anything else I can do that won't make enough noise to wake her. I don't want her family coming anywhere near our bedroom or offices upstairs, but I straighten up what I can, regardless. I shove a few things into the closet in my office, smiling when I see the pile of Christmas gifts waiting there.

Tomorrow is going to be hard for both of us. Me, because I'm going to confront Alexander and end this once and for all. Her, because she's confronting her asshole family for the first time in years. Both of us are going to be overwrought.

But Christmas will be just us. I'll make sure she sleeps in, and wake her up with an orgasm or two, and then we can have a leisurely day opening presents and kissing by the fire and eating leftovers from her Christmas Eve party. It's exactly what we both deserve.

Chores complete for now, I return to bed, slipping inside to hold Casey. Still perfectly asleep, she turns right into my hold, snuggling close. She trusts me to keep her safe and warm.

I'll keep her safe and warm until the day I die, which, if I have my way, will be a very long time from now. After all, she's the entire reason my heart even beats, so it only seems fair.

I bury my nose in her hair, breathing in her presence in an attempt to convince my body to succumb to the exhaustion I should feel.

Unfortunately, my brain won't stop turning over the day. Alexander, and whoever that larger panther I killed was, and the kid, Jacob. And there had been the training ground, too—maybe he did sell those kids on to whoever funds his sick experiments, but maybe he has his own little miniature army waiting for me.

I can take an army. I have before, slicing through throngs of mindless thugs to get to a target that Luc needed eliminated. It's not the numbers that bother me.

But what if they're kids like Jacob? Could I kill a whole host of kids? I haven't killed a kid since I was one myself, and I try very hard not to think about that.

Casey huffs, and I settle, forcing myself to breathe deeply. She smells like the lavender from that bath bomb and something about that centers me, letting me put the problem in perspective.

I almost get out of bed to call Luc. A quick glance at the clock tells me it's after eleven now, but he'll pick up. I've earned that over the years, the assumption that I won't waste his time, that if I call for him, it's damned important. He'll pick up.

He'll give me the answers I need, too, because nothing is ever accomplished if the man needing the information only knows half the story. Luc keeps his secrets, but he's very good at knowing when to start doling them out.

I could go back into my office and make the call. It might even settle my mind, giving it something productive to turn over.

I squeeze Casey slightly. In the morning. I'll solve all this first thing in the morning.

December 24th, 6:30 am

Well, not first thing in the morning. There's only one valid way to start the day around here, after all.

When my face is dripping with her come and I've made sure we've both eaten—since I never remembered to make her eat her bagel last night—I kiss her goodbye, promise again to pick up the ham, and drive to the governor's office.

"You've been tracking Alexander the whole time," I say, forgoing a greeting entirely as I walk into his office.

Luc, to his credit, doesn't even flinch. "Of course I have," he agrees. "He's the biggest threat to us. You think I was just going to let him go?"

I pause for a moment, re-formulating my thoughts, then sit down across from him. "You never told me."

"Why would I do that? He wasn't your responsibility." He seems genuinely perplexed, or as perplexed as someone like Luc can sound. He never quite lets it show of course, too determined to be entirely in control, but I know him. I've always known him.

"You didn't think I'd want to know?" I challenge him.

He pushes his papers aside, giving me his full attention. "There's no point in telling you just to distract you. You had your own tasks."

"You knew." It's a stupid argument, because of course he knew. But I don't know how to explain that I expect more from him. That I've been with him since the beginning, that I've known him the longest. That I always assumed my position here was a step above everyone else. That I assumed he trusted me.

"It's my job to know," he sighs. "I organize it all, Max. I keep all the pieces moving in the right direction."

"If Alexander is our toughest enemy, the most dangerous threat, then shouldn't I have been aware?" I ask. "I handle the most dangerous threats."

"Could you have handled this one?"

"I'm handling it, aren't I?" I snap. A delay doesn't mean I fucking failed. He should trust me to still get the job done.

"Yes, because there's something in it for you now. Something you value more than anything. But before Casey came along..." He trails off for a moment, organizing his thoughts, and I wait with the very last of my patience. "Could you have faced Alexander? And disobeyed any direct order he gave you?"

That stings. "What the fuck does that mean?"

"I chose you because you were his best soldier," he snaps back at me, clearly running out of patience for my obtuseness. "Not only would you be better trained, more lethal, more useful as a partner, but taking you would also strike a decisive blow to him. How was he going to come after us without you? You were his greatest weapon, Maximus. And you did what he told you."

We all did, or we died. So what if I was better at staying alive than most of us were? That doesn't mean that I'm loyal to Alexander.

"Fuck you, Luc," I tell him, keeping my voice as even as I can. "Tell me everything."

He raises an eyebrow. "Do you make demands now?"

Luc gave me my life. He gave me the chance to survive long enough to meet Casey and truly live. I've spent every day aware of how much I owe him.

But he needs me too. And if absolutely nothing else can be said between us, if our history really is worth so little, then the very least I can say is he's smart enough to understand that a well-informed weapon is a more useful weapon.

"Tell me," I repeat.

He looks at me for just a second before nodding. "You know he hasn't stopped," he says. "Every time we turn around, we find more." He means the rest of his loyal band of followers. There's about twenty of them, from all different ages in history. I'm ashamed to admit it's the first time I've considered what happened to the rest of their litters. That they surely were not made alone.

"So you've, what?" I ask, setting that aside firmly to think about later.

"I've put plans in place. Some of us actively seek him out, Max. As my influence grew, I could put pressure on others to turn him in. It's been slow-going, but I never expected otherwise. You know I'm always here for the long game."

Yeah, that I know. It had taken centuries for him to get what he was after, and I doubt he's done now. But he's never complained, never wavered. He's just kept pushing towards the future he planned for himself.

"Who does he even sell them to?" I demand.

Luc shrugs. "If I knew that, I would have found him centuries ago. Near as I can tell, it's a mix. Sometimes they're bought by supernatural creatures. There's always plenty of fighting behind the scenes. Regime changes, power plays. But you and I cut into a lot of that business, so Alexander had to get creative. So sometimes they're bought by who you'd expect to be looking for soldiers in modern day wars. No different than what would have happened to us, really."

"Are you telling me the human military is buying specially bred soldiers that can shift into animals?" I ask incredulously. "That they know?"

Sure, we had been sold to the Roman Emperor, so I knew Alexander wasn't above involving humans. But in those days, a wild animal appearing mid-battle to take out the opposing army could be explained as divine intervention. I doubt that excuse works these days.

Luc shrugs. "It's not like every grunt knows who they're fighting alongside. I'd guess the information is kept very secret, that only those at the very top would know. And they're human, Max. Easy to take out and replace if things go wrong. But humans pay a pretty penny for weapons their enemies don't have in war. If Alexander is playing both sides, he could make out very, very well."

An understatement. A sick feeling takes me over. "Have you considered it?"

He looks amused for a half a second, but more in a rehearsed way than anything I'd believe is genuine. It's a look he probably practices in the mirror before campaign stops. "Are you asking if I'd personally buy enhanced super soldier slaves to fill out my army? I know you're upset that I didn't tell you everything going on, Max, but I promise I didn't manage to keep a secret army controlled by the governor from you."

Yeah, maybe not. But we all know he's gunning for president next. And that does come with the title of Commander-in-Chief.

He must see the continued doubt on my face, because he softens slightly. "I would die before buying anything from Alexander," he says firmly.

I know I'm just a grunt. I know that I've followed Luc's lead for two millennia now. But even I can tell that's a crafted, political answer. I raise an eyebrow, and he sighs. "I don't make promises for a future we haven't reached yet, Max."

"Bullshit. I met a kid yesterday who was our age when we escaped. Couldn't grow a damned beard, no muscle on his frame yet. Alexander handed him a shotgun and when I broke his arm taking it away from him, Alexander threatened to put him down like a dog. I don't know if he lived or not."

"Not like you to care about anyone other than that girl of yours," he observes, tone infuriatingly mild.

"My wife is the center of my universe, and I'm willing to give you basically everything for her," I shoot back, unable to maintain the same level of calm. "But I don't think she'd like me killing fucking kids."

The thought of Jacob makes me sick. Could I kill him if it was a choice between him and Casey? Absolutely. It's amazing what I could make myself do if it's for her. But I don't think I'd live comfortably with myself for a long while.

"You used to kill kids all the time."

All the time seems like an unfair exaggeration, and it's not like I'd chosen it. "I was a kid," I mutter, my blood turning to sludge in my veins at the thought. "I wanted to live."

Luc just stares at me for a long moment. "I'm no better," he admits quietly, the most vulnerable and honest I've heard him be in centuries, probably. "I did what I had to. Anyone who walked out of there did."

Luc looks small and weak, but really, he's just small. Maybe he can't snap a trained soldier's neck as quickly as I can, but he never needed to.

Luc fights dirty, going for arteries and weak points, using sticks and stones and whatever else was at hand. He moves fast too. And once he'd discovered poison, it was all over.

"I'm not criticizing you for surviving, Max," he says, although it sure as fuck had sounded like that. "I'm pointing out the flaw in your suddenly sanctimonious logic. You've always been a pragmatist, a survivor. Don't stop now. We don't know what will be down the road next year, or in five, or ten. We'll do what we need to survive. But I can promise you I'll never buy a single soul from Alexander."

It's still too weak of a promise, but I nod anyway. Luc is in charge. Luc makes these decisions, and it's just my job to execute them.

It's silent for a long moment, but then Luc steeples his fingers. "You have a plan to find him?"

Plan puts too fine a point on it. Plan sounds far too deliberate.

I nod regardless. "I'll get him."

December 24th, 10:30 am

I start by going back to the training pit I found in the woods yesterday.

The stench of bodies buried in shallow graves nearby almost ruins my ability to track anything else, but I haven't survived this long by giving up. I scent carefully, looking for signs of Alexander or either of the two shifters I met yesterday.

They haven't been here recently, and I didn't expect them to come back. But it's at least a place to start tracking them from.

I move through the woods on auto-pilot, allowing my wolf form to lower his nose to the ground and track the scent, and I think about what needs to happen next. There can be no talking today, because there's no bargaining with someone like Alexander. The plan is simple. Find him, beat him to a pulp, grab him, and torture the information I need out of him. Take down anyone who stands in my way. Show him exactly what he made me, and exactly what a mistake he made, unleashing a creature like me on the world.

The trail of scent gets stronger, and when I investigate, it's immediately obvious why. Another training pit.

It takes a lot of training to make something like me. I know from experience. It takes a lot of time to make those animal instincts come to the forefront, to make a boy willingly rip out the throat of another without blinking. It takes a lot to make them shake off any amount of pain, to keep going, and to prize mission objectives over their own lives, over their friend's lives.

I am the product of that, and, no matter what Luc says about me, there's still a part of me that gets sick thinking of the other boys who are going through that now.

Or not going through it. Training like that, not everyone makes it through. That's the point; only the most ruthless, the strongest, the most controllable, survive. And there's another grave here, over under the old oak tree.

Alexander wouldn't take the time to bury one of his soldiers like that, and my heart actually hurts for the kids who had to bury their friend.

I'd been the one to do that once. I'd killed them because I'd had to, and then I'd buried them.

Fuck, I haven't thought about that in years.

They're not here, and I'm not here to revisit the horrors of the past. I'm here to get answers, to get a future for Casey and myself, and, if I'm lucky, get Alexander's mangled body to drag back to Luc.

Nose to the ground, I keep moving. There's a path that leads back towards the farmhouse I torched yesterday, and I ignore that one, instead tracking a path that smells like the panther I killed yesterday. There's another scent under it, a little fainter—lynx, I think, and I have to wonder how many litters Alexander ran through here, or if he's breeding more than one group at a time now.

Or maybe he's diversifying. We were all wolves, but I have no idea how or why that came about. Maybe he gets to choose, or maybe there are different components to the spell he can swap out, depending on what he's hoping for.

And then a wall of muscle hits me from the side.

Fuck. I spare half a thought to think maybe the training to let our animal instincts completely take over has some merit, because no way the me of two thousand years ago would have been so distracted by useless thoughts that he gets blindsided by an attack. Then I growl and roll, trying to force my opponent underneath the wolf.

A wolf's bite strength can tear through bone without that much trouble, and I aim to take out the paw across my throat. My attacker pulls back before my teeth can close around him, which gives me room to push to my feet, bringing me up to full force and growling loud enough that the trees around us shake with the rumble of it.

I'm a fierce, scary motherfucker. Creatures like us have lived in fear of me for centuries. I am the monster under the bed. And I want to make sure this fucker knows it. I will rip his limbs off and do it slowly, just to make a point.

I'm faced with a bear. Not a normal bear, of course, because I've never seen a normal grizzly bear with quite so much murder in their eyes. Not to mention the lingering smell of human beneath the bear, the scent that sets all of Alexander's experiments apart from the rest of the world.

I lunge at the bear, determined to get this over with quickly. I must be on the right trail if Alexander is sending his soldiers to stop me. He's a fool for it, of course, because I was always his best and I've only gotten better with time. But maybe he's desperate. That's just how I want him, and this bear isn't going to stop me from getting to him quickly.

He swipes at me when I get close, and I turn, taking the rake of claws across my shoulder instead of my neck. The pain forces a growl out of me, but other than that, I ignore it. Pain is just a distraction.

I jump on the bear's back, listening to him roar and holding tight as he tries to shake me off. It's a close thing, because wolves don't exactly have thumbs, but I hold on and get my jaw around his neck.

Blood fills my mouth, but I don't let go until at last the bear is limp under me.

I spit out the blood, surveying the corpse I left behind. Fuck Alexander for sending this one after me. He knew he had no chance.

It just means I'm getting close, though. It has to. No one wastes resources defending things that don't matter.

I give the wounds on my shoulder a cursory check. They're still bleeding freely, but they'll heal on their own if given enough time. They'll hurt something awful in the meantime, but I don't give a fuck. I have a job to complete, and Casey, whether or not she knows it, is depending on me to do it. I can't fail her.

Judging by the sun, it's noon when I stop again. Fuck, I promised Casey I'd only work a half day today. I should turn back to my car and at least call her, but that would require letting go of all this progress.

She'll forgive me. I'll beg for it if I have to, and I won't let her down. I'll return home in time for her party with our future secured.

The problem is that I'm not getting any closer. I haven't lost the scent, but it keeps crisscrossing, and I have a sinking suspicion that it's all on purpose, that this was laid as a decoy for me. The panther I killed yesterday's scent is obviously old, but the bear I just killed and the lynx I smelled earlier weave in and out, going this way and that. If I was a human, I'd be turned in circles, hopelessly lost.

I'm on high alert, waiting for another attack to come from the shadows. What will it be this time? A fucking snake shifter? A moose? What even are the rules of these transformations, anyway?

The path goes up a hill, and I put my nose to the ground, suddenly moving faster, because now I scent another person who I'm too familiar with. It's probably some sort of trick, something to throw me off, but I have to try, anyway.

But when I crest the hill, Alexander is standing at the top, a long staff in hand that I know from experience is much more for hitting than it is for magic.

"You were looking for me," he says, his voice as smug and infuriating as he could possibly be, like he already knew, already predicted what I would do.

Fuck. Him.

I don't waste time talking or answering his question. There's nothing he'll tell me, not now. People like Alexander only respect strength. He won't give me anything until he knows he has no other option. And that's fine with me. I am what he made me, and I relish the idea of breaking a few of his bones along the way.

I lunge for him, already calculating a few steps ahead. He'll turn into my attack, and I'll get my jaw around his arm. If he's smart and pulls backwards, I can still get my jaw around his leg. I'll dig in and break the bone, and I won't let go until the fight leaves him. Then I can take my human form back and land a few good punches before I drag him back to my car.

He raises that damned stick to protect himself. I grab it, wrenching it away from him, snapping it between my jaws and throwing the pieces away, but it buys him the seconds he needs.

"Now," he snaps, and I can smell them before I see them. A half a dozen fucking creatures, a whole damned zoo, pouring out of the surrounding trees.

What the fuck had Alexander done to me, that I couldn't sense them? I can smell a drop of Casey's blood when she gets a paper cut in her office and I'm in the kitchen. There shouldn't be anything that would prevent me from sensing them.

My shock buys them the second they need. The lynx is the fastest, followed by another bear. I stand at my fullest height and let out a growl that should shake their very bones, hoping to remind them what they're facing.

But if they're Alexander's latest projects, then they don't know any better. They haven't been exposed to the world enough to know to fear me, and regardless, Alexander will have long since beaten the fear out of them.

I rip the throat out of the lynx, then the bear, but by the time I stand upright from that attack, a panther is almost on me. It's not Jacob; my brain has enough time to recognize that before I'm embroiled in another fight, and my opponent is faster than me and fresher, too.

Still, I can handle three opponents. The panther dies like the others, but only after cleaving a bloody gash down my flank.

Fuck. I turn, growling loudly, ready to face whoever is next.

A bear remains in front of Alexander, guarding my prey from me. I advance, breaking into the fastest run I can manage with the wounds I have, ready to barrel into the bear and hopefully take him by surprise. Eliminate the bear, take Alexander. Torture him for the information I need.

The bear draws up on its hind legs, going to its fullest height, and I lunge, jumping upward, ready to end this now.

And then there's pain lacing through my spine. Something hit me from behind.

I whine, my limbs losing control, as I fall and crash to the ground. I try to force myself up, try to make myself move, but I can't get my limbs under control.

My heart beats faster, a fear I've never felt before sending my blood racing. Not now. Not like this. Casey is expecting me at home tonight. I'm supposed to pick up the ham and support her when her family is there. I have Christmas presents for her tomorrow. I'm supposed to make us hot chocolate and kiss her in front of the fire all day long. This cannot be how it ends. Not when I didn't get to tell her the truth. Not when I didn't actually get to be her husband.

Alexander's face looms over mine. "Maybe you'll get up and maybe you won't," he says conversationally. "I doubt it, but you always surprised me, and you know me, Maximus: I'm a big proponent of surviving—or not—on your own merits. If you do live, tell your boss this is what happens when you cross me. If his best tool couldn't take me, then what chance does he have?"

He leans close, kneeling down now. I can still move my mouth, so I try to snap at him, but I can't move my neck to reach him.

He chuckles. "And Maximus? You might be the tool, but I'll punish you on your own merits. And I always make sure my punishments fit the crime. You messed with my business. I'll pay you back tenfold. Think of that."

And then he touches my neck. I can't suppress my whine—I don't want his fucking hands anywhere near me—but he ignores me. He grabs my neck and then twists.

And then it all goes black.

December 24th, 4:30pm

When I wake up, the sun is setting, and everything fucking hurts. It's like knives are under my skin, prying under my nerves, sending fire shooting along my body.

Hurting is actually a good sign, I realize after a prolonged moment of misery. It means my body is in the process of healing from the paralysis.

The sun setting absolutely isn't a good thing. I told Casey it would be a half day. I was supposed to pick up the ham and be home in time to help her finish her preparations and keep her as calm as possible. Instead, I'm naked in the woods, probably unable to walk, and so furiously angry at myself that I'm surprised I don't spontaneously combust. Fucking fuck. I didn't even know it was possible to fuck up this badly.

I test my limbs, and it feels like someone poured razors into my bloodstream even just when twitching a finger. I take deep breaths through my nose. Okay, that doesn't matter. It'll keep getting better, and I can handle a little pain.

The plan is simple: get back to my car, get clean clothes from the trunk, pick up the ham, and think of how to apologize to Casey for being late as I break a few traffic laws speeding home. Then, tomorrow, regroup with Luc about what the hell to do about Alexander. Simple, straightforward. Any idiot can do that.

I can't make myself get up.

A scream erupts from my throat, brutal and piercing and loud enough to shake the trees. It's like it all boils over, every frustration, every bit of pain. And then I force myself to stand.

I'm shaking like a leaf from the pain, but I make myself take one step, then another. It gets better, and I can't tell if I'm getting used to it, or if the healing is continuing to work.

I look down the hill. I have a pretty solid sense of direction, even in my human form, and I know for a fact that my car is nowhere near here. It'll be faster to get there in wolf form.

I grit my teeth. This is going to suck.

I have to stop in a stream on the way back to bathe and check myself when I get to the car once more to make sure there aren't any sticks or leaves in my hair. The scratches littering my skin haven't faded yet, but the shirt I have in the trunk is at least long-sleeved.

The ham is waiting for me, and I'm just damned grateful that the restaurant isn't closed yet. I'm not really physically up for performing a break-in to get Casey the ham. I would have tried it, though, pain or no pain. She deserves a man who keeps his promises, no matter what.

It's close to seven when I pull into our driveway. I can't get to my usual spot; someone has already parked there.

They've been here for an hour already, probably. There's an untold amount of damage they could have done in an hour.

My steps are still a little unsteady as I let myself in, but I doubt it's noticeable. Fuck, I hope it's not noticeable.

Casey's face lights up like the fucking sun when she sees me. Not even a hint of anger, and fuck, she's too good. She should be furious, especially because I don't have a good excuse that I can give her. She should be pissed off and punish me somehow, give me the cold shoulder or at least a sound telling-off.

Maybe she's just so happy to see a friendly face in this crowd.

I look her over. She looks damned good, and I spare half a second to wonder how long she spent getting ready before I let the thought go and just appreciate it.

She has her curls half up, half spilling over her neck. She doesn't wear makeup most days, but she has it on today, and it makes those brown eyes look even bigger, those long lashes somehow impossibly longer.

And her dress. That fucking dress.

It's a long sleeve sweater dress, a creamy white that looks soft to the touch. She has opaque red tights under it, so every inch of skin is hidden. Probably to hide her tattoos from her parents, and I'd be upset that she has to do that if I wasn't so focused on how that dress hugs every single curve. I am going to have the hardest time keeping my hands to myself tonight.

And I know my girl. She's never done anything halfway in her life, and I bet there's some sort of delicious surprise just for me under that dress. Casey likes online shopping when she's in a certain mood, and she always finds the most beautiful things.

A throat clears. "You must be Max."

Fuck, right. The guests she dressed for in the first place. "I am," I agree, turning my attention unwillingly from Casey to the guests in our living room.

Her father is a judge, and the man's serious expression makes me think he's casting judgment right now. I get the feeling he doesn't like me much. That's okay; I don't like him much either.

His wife's dress would fit right into a Stepford Wives shot, and her careful makeup makes it hard to tell how old she actually is. The only reason I assume she's Casey's mother and not the sister-in-law is because the sister-in-law is loosely holding hands with the younger man.

Her brother, the family's golden child. Harvard law school, a prestigious law firm that protects only the most corrupt millionaires, and is now supposedly a future senator. I wonder if he knows Luc.

I should have asked Luc if he had any dirt on this guy.

I paste a smile on my face, and I hope only Casey can tell that it's fake. "I apologize for being late," I say. "Got held up at the state house."

"State house is closed today," Casey's brother says.

"Not for the governor."

That word has the effect I expected it to, and eyes turn to me, more curious than hostile. I hoist the bag in my hand. "Casey, sorry I'm late. I brought dinner."

"I thought you were cooking," her mother says.

Shit. I didn't realize the ham was a secret, although I probably should have.

"I did cook," Casey says, her voice oddly inflectionless. "Just didn't want to make a whole ham. I'll help you, Max."

As soon as we're around the corner into the kitchen, I pull her into a kiss. She kisses me back, but pulls away after a moment, one hand resting on my chest. "Where have you been? Is everything okay?"

I take a deep breath, inhaling the scent of her. I'm doing great now. I couldn't care less that I still ache, or that there's a group of assholes in our living room. Anything is bearable with Casey here.

"I'm okay. I'm sorry. Something—something came up," I say. It's a poor excuse.

She doesn't let me get away with it, either. And I'm glad Casey isn't taking my bullshit or anyone else's, but fuck, I don't want to have to double-down on my lie. "You didn't answer your phone."

It's been in my car all day, and when I'd gotten back to the car, I hadn't bothered to check it, just driven home as fast as I could. "Forgot it in the car."

She raises an eyebrow, clearly still not impressed. "I've already listened to twenty minutes from Jennifer about how you're definitely cheating on me."

Fuck. That. I know she doesn't believe it, but I need to squash any doubt lingering in her mind immediately. I set the bag with our dinner aside, then grab her by the hips. Heedless of the pain in my still-healing body, I lift her, planting that perfect ass on the counter and stepping between her thighs so I can kiss her stupid, letting my fingers sink into the soft fabric of her dress.

She wrinkles my shirt, trying to drag me closer, kissing with a desperate sort of hunger. She doesn't believe whatever nonsense her sister-in-law is saying, but she knows something is going on, and I can feel her confusion in her kiss.

"I'm sorry, baby," I tell her, doing my best to stroke her dress back into place even if all I want is to ruck it up over her hips. "I promise I wouldn't have stayed away unless it was important."

"I know," she tells me, then wiggles until I help her down from the counter. "Let's get dinner served. I don't want them to wait any longer."

I put my hands on her hips as she tries to walk away from me. "How have they been?" I keep my voice low, not wanting them to overhear from the next room, but I need to get a feel for where we're at. I won't let them disrespect Casey. I won't let them make tonight more difficult for her.

She makes a face, all the answers that I need, and I nod. Alright. Dinner's goal is defense, then.

Together, we plate up six servings, pulling dishes out of the oven where Casey had them on low to keep them warm, plating the ham which, thankfully, looks delicious and no worse for wear for having to wait for me to pick it up.

"Dinner is served," she says, walking back into the living room. Her voice is so carefully neutral and I know that took practice. It's practice I'd hoped she'd forgotten, too, but evidently not.

"About time. Casey, it's rude to keep your guests waiting. For future reference, dinner should ideally start thirty to forty minutes after your guest arrives. And you should really have hors d'oeuvres prepared for when your guests are waiting."

I grit my teeth. "Dinner being late is my fault," I remind Casey's mother politely. "I'm sorry, Mrs. Jackson. Let's eat now. The food is hot and smells delicious."

And I know for a fact that Casey spent all day working on it, although I don't say that. I don't want to hear how they'd respond.

We never eat at our dining room table, but I'm glad we have it for tonight. I can picture these people turning up their nose at being made to eat at a kitchen table, despite a table literally being a table, and making no damn difference to the quality of food.

I pull out a chair for Casey at the head of the table, helping her in. She gives me a small, private smile that makes my heart beat a little faster. I want to bend over and give her a kiss, but I can feel her family watching us, so I refrain for now.

I'm probably supposed to sit at the other end of the table, but I couldn't give less of a fuck. Whoever made that rule didn't like their spouse very much, because I fully plan on sitting right next to Casey. She's the only person at this dinner party I have any desire to spend time with.

Her brother sits on her other side, her sister-in-law next to him. Her mother sits next to me, and her father takes the seat at the other end of the table, across from his daughter.

"Ham is for Easter," her mother sniffs. "Beef for Christmas, darling."

I'm vividly reminded that I'd called her darling exactly once, on our third or fourth date, and she'd gotten too quiet after. I'd never tried to use that endearment again.

I nudge her foot with mine beneath the table, just so she's reminded that I'm here. "I like ham," I tell them, even though I don't have any particular affinity for it. Food is food, really. But if they're going to blame anyone—especially for something so fucking stupid—then they can blame me.

The silence is uncomfortable for a long moment, but then her brother turns to me. "So, you work for the governor," he says with interest in his eyes.

No doubt Brian Jackson thinks I'm a leg-up in whatever future career aspirations he has. This is a man who has never once bothered to call his sister, not even on her birthday. But he'll use her husband as a stepping-stone in his career without an ounce of shame.

"I do," I agree, trying to keep my voice neutral.

"What do you do?"

There's a story Luc and I worked out, an official job title that comes with having an actual paying job in his office. "I'm in public outreach." My tone doesn't invite further questions. It's accurate enough, too. I do reach out to the public. Only I don't solicit votes or policy change. I'm the muscle, the intimidation. I'm what keeps the public in line. Not that I'll be sharing that with anyone present anytime soon.

"Interesting," Jennifer says, lowering her fork from perfectly red lips. "That must be a worthwhile job."

I can't tell if worthwhile is a backhanded compliment or not, and I'm not super interested in finding out. "Yeah, it's fine," I tell them. "Doesn't take quite as much creativity as Casey's work though. Now, what she does is always exciting. And it's beautiful."

Everyone at the table turns to her for a moment, and she shrinks from their gazes. My gut clenches at the sight.

"Indeed," her father says. "Art has always been an interesting career choice."

Art. Like he's not really sure exactly what she does, so he says art to cover all his bases. Like he realized early on that his daughter was talented in something he didn't understand, so he simply gave up on caring.

Casey is a kick-ass graphic designer. She makes logos and flyers and websites and even does layouts for magazines and books sometimes. Last month she did a layout for a travel book that was so beautiful I wished desperately to take her there. She sees things with color that I could never understand. If it wasn't blatant nepotism, I'd beg for her to design everything to do with Luc's office.

But yeah, okay. Art, like it could be interchanged with a curse.

I take a bite so I don't say anything. "Dinner is delicious, Casey," I say, turning fully to her and giving her a smile so she knows I'm sincere.

"Thank you," she murmurs, voice still too-quiet. "I—"

Her mother cuts her off. "So, tell us about work, Brian."

And Brian proceeds to detail what seems like his every waking moment. Casey's career gets brushed off with *interesting career choice* in her own home, but Brian gets the chance to narrate every single thought he's had in the last two weeks.

What's worse is, from what Casey told me, Brian sees his parents regularly. That's always the complaint when Casey makes herself call them—Brian visits regularly, and Casey ignores them. So they've seen Brian recently, and they finally get a moment with Casey, but they don't want to talk to her.

And Casey sits quietly through it all. I nudge her foot with mine again, then reach over and briefly touch the back of her hand, just so she knows she's not alone.

Everything in me screams to throw these people out of our house. That they're here, endangering the peace Casey and I have built, and they're a threat to us. That they shouldn't be allowed anywhere near Casey. I want them gone, and the wolf in me is more than eager to drag them out myself.

But Casey invited them here, knowing exactly what they'd be like, and I can't remove them without her say-so. She wanted this, knowing it wouldn't be fun or easy. It's important to her. So I eat another bite of my food and bite my tongue.

Finally, when Brian finishes telling us every minute detail of his frankly very boring life, they all seem to remember that they're in someone else's home. "So, Max, do you know the governor personally?" Casey's father asks.

"He's my oldest friend, Mr. Jackson," I say. It's mostly truthful, too, although I'm not sure that either Luc or I have a typical working definition of friend.

We've never tried to kill each other since we escaped Alexander. That has to count for something.

"Really?" Mrs. Jackson leans forward now, interest apparent in her eyes like a shark. I know this woman is a housewife, but I suddenly think her son gets his predatory lawyer tendencies from her rather than his father. "Casey, how interesting. You never mentioned that."

"Have you met him?" Brian asks her, the first words I've heard him say directly to his sister.

"We've had dinner," Casey says, voice still quiet, and she barely looks up from her plate even though a quick glance confirms that she's scarcely eaten anything.

Fuck, would the Jacksons be more welcoming to Casey if I got Brian a meeting with Luc? Appeasement isn't usually how I solve my problems, but I'd be willing to give it a try if it smoothes the way for Casey.

I'm just about to open my mouth and suggest it—maybe a casual dinner, or even a lunch, just the three of us—when Mrs. Jackson goes and proves to me why I don't waste my time with appeasement.

"Well, I hope you dressed better, Casey. You're not a teenager anymore, darling, and that dress doesn't project a very sophisticated image. We're proud of you for finding yourself a respectable man, but if you're going to enter this world, then you need to act like it."

Okay, that's it. I don't know if it's just one snide comment too many, or the implication that I'm respectable when Casey somehow isn't, but I can't do this anymore.

"Do not talk about my wife like that." The words come out cold as ice, and usually that tone is a precursor to sudden death. Unfortunately, no one at this table knows my reputation in that regard, but that's alright. I can enlighten them.

Mr. Jackson's jaw hangs open. "Your wife?" he demands.

I ignore it. "Casey wowed Luc when they met. Because she's goddamn impressive in all circumstances. People should be lucky to know her; I know I fucking am."

Her father bristles. "Listen, young man—"

I'm older than him by an order of magnitude, but that's irrelevant. "You don't come into our home and treat your daughter like that. You might have been enough of a sack of shit to do it in your home, but not in ours."

"This is getting blown out of proportion," Mrs. Jackson says, a falsely sweet note in her voice now, the consummate peace-maker, trained to smooth over other people's messes. "You live in a tough world, son. And Casey hasn't always shown she's the most prepared for it. This is just motherly concern."

I do live in a tough world, and she doesn't know the half of it. But Casey is fully prepared for it, because I will always be at her side. If she needs a man willing to do bad things for her, then I'll be right there. And I might have never known my mother, but I know for certain that whatever this is and motherly concern exist in entirely separate universes.

"Keep your concern to yourself."

I'm radiating anger, and smart creatures should know to be weary of me because cornered wolves snap when antagonized.

Unfortunately, these people are not smart creatures. If they had been, they would have recognized their daughter for the gem she is a long time ago. And they never would have dared to speak ill of her in front of me.

"Son—" Mr. Jackson begins.

Casey cuts him off. She's looking entirely at her plate, but her voice is firm, regardless. "Don't talk to him like that," she says. "He's not your son. He's a grown man and this is our house and you don't get to come in here and belittle him. At least have the courtesy to use his name when you're talking to him."

Of course she'd use every bit of energy she has to fight defending me, regardless of whether or not I need it. My heart squeezes.

"Darling—" her mother tries.

Casey interrupts. "I have a name too. Use it."

It's silent for a long, pregnant moment. "Casey," her mother tries again.

I can tell from the look on Casey's face that Casey isn't much better than darling, not when it's said in her mother's voice. But she doesn't argue again.

I wait for Mrs. Jackson to say whatever she's going to say, ready to pick up the fight for the both of us if need be. My wife will never be left to defend us on her own.

Only she doesn't say anything. I think for a moment that Casey's firm retort has actually stunned her family into behaving appropriately, but then Casey's face goes slack, and then I feel the shift in the room.

The air feels like soup, like everything around us is slow and thick. "Fuck," I murmur, immediately grabbing for Casey. I don't know what this is, but I know I want to be between whatever it is and her.

There's a crash behind us, and I instinctively turn to face it. Our front door is smashed to pieces, and I'm torn between running to confront whoever thinks breaking into my house is a good idea and staying right here, right in front of Casey.

Needing to protect Casey wins out. I don't move, planting myself between her and the entrance to the dining room.

She squeezes my hand. "Max? What is it?" she asks, fear permeating her words. "Why are my parents..." She doesn't finish her sentence, and I don't turn to check on them, instead just watching for whatever is coming for us.

It's Alexander, flanked by the two shifters from this morning that I didn't manage to kill. "Well, that is interesting," he says, looking over my shoulder. I shift to fully block Casey from his eyes, but it's too late. "The beast really did find his fragile little beauty. I told you I'd make the lesson stick this time, Max. And you just gave me such a tool."

"Get out of my home," I say, reluctantly dropping Casey's hand. "If you value your life, leave."

He tsks, stepping closer like he doesn't have a single concern in the entire world. "We already know you want to kill me, Maximus. And we already know that you've failed at it. So let's not waste time on useless threats. I'm simply ensuring you understand the message."

He turns to the man on his left. "Start with the girl," he says. "The others aren't going anywhere." A darting glance confirms that the rest of the family is sitting around like they were frozen in ice. Their eyes, wide and alert, are the only sign that they're not simply dolls. My stomach clenches. What kind of fucking magic is this?

I reach for Casey again, pushing her back. I've never had to fight like this before, with someone actually worth defending at my back. I'm calculating how to best get her out of the room to somewhere safe when Alexander's man decides I'm out of time. He lunges, and I'm torn for half a second between shifting to fight better and staying human to protect my secret from Casey.

Fuck it. Casey can hate me later, but I won't risk her life. I shift to my wolf form, taking the attack head on, growling and blocking the attack from reaching Casey. It's my worst fear come true, to see someone look at her with that type of intention. But I won't let them anywhere near her. I'll die before I let them touch a hair on her head.

My fucking woman. And nothing on this planet is going to hurt her.

"What the fuck!" Casey nearly shouts, and it pains me to do it, but I have to ignore her and her fear and her panic, because if I focus on her, then I won't be able to keep her safe.

"Careful there," Alexander calls. "Leave the little mortal alone too long, and the spell will make it easy to grab her right up."

"Max," Casey pleads, fear evident in her voice.

I growl and snap at my opponent. He hasn't shifted yet, and I realize why when he draws a knife.

A knife would never be enough to make me afraid, except for today, because I'm acutely aware of who else is in the room. And Casey can be hurt by a knife.

I snap his wrist clean through. Let him try to use a knife on her now.

I expected some sort of reaction from Casey to that, considering the level of violence. When she doesn't make so much as a peep, I whirl to face her.

She's as frozen as her family now, wide, fearful eyes watching me even as she can't move. I whine, rushing over to her, heedless of the threats behind us in my determination to get to her.

I nudge at her outstretched hand. Fuck, was she reaching for me? Even like this?

As soon as I touch her, the spell breaks, and the hand I'm nudging reflexively tightens in my fur. I never let anyone touch me in my wolf form and live to tell about it, but I decide right here and now that Casey can touch my fur whenever she wants.

It's not the fucking time for that, I remind myself, because there are still active threats in this room.

Alexander claps a few times, a mocking tilt to his face as he watches her. Casey tightens her fingers in my fur, unconsciously seeking me for protection against danger, and that makes my heart leap a bit. That's right, sweetheart. I'm yours.

I'm your monster, and I'll bite out the heart of anyone who scares you.

Unable to say that to her in the wolf form, I hold the thought and hope she knows.

"Bravo, Maximus. You finally learned to put others over yourself, hm?"

I growl, lips pulled back to reveal my teeth. Sadly, Alexander is more than used to the antics of discontented shifters, so he barely acknowledges it. The only thing this man is going to respect is death.

I have to leave Casey's side, because the fucker is trying to lead me away. I lunge at him as fast as I can, trying to draw his full attention to me. Then I change the angle of my lunge at the last second so I can take down Alexander.

He slams to the ground under the weight of the wolf, and I bring my teeth to his neck. He has the gall to laugh under me. "Careful," he wheezes. "Leaving your pet awfully vulnerable, aren't you?"

I lift my head to make eye-contact with the shifter approaching a once-again frozen Casey and growl with enough force that it should shake his bones. Instead, he reaches out and grabs Casey.

"No, you fool—" It's too late. His touch unfreezes Casey just as effectively as mine did, her terrified scream ringing through the house.

Before I can get to her, she picks up a knife from the table and stabs her assailant through the shoulder.

The knife is meant to cut meat and not a man, and certainly not a supernaturally enhanced man. I wince, knowing all she's done is piss him off. He looks at the knife, then at her. And I see her flinch when she realizes what deep shit she's in.

But my brave girl does the only thing she can do, smart enough to work out that running won't get her very far; she picks up a second knife, and feints with it, ready to try again.

So I do the only thing I can do. I transform back to a man as quickly as I can, then snap Alexander's neck, like he did to me earlier.

Let him walk away from that anytime soon. If I can still feel a twinge from earlier, I'm confident I can keep Alexander on the ground until Luc can get here.

"Hey, fuckhead," I snarl. Talking during fights is for people who can't finish them, but I need this man's attention away from Casey. He half-turns, and I lunge.

I don't allow myself to hesitate, using the element of surprise to my fullest advantage. He tries to shift once I get my hands around him, but I'm faster.

I tear his throat open with my bare hands, uncaring as he gurgles under me in surprise, panting as I watch his cooling corpse.

Still straddling the corpse on the floor, I look up towards Casey, only to find her frozen again, knife outstretched towards me.

"It's going to be okay, sweetheart," I say as gently as I can, standing and stepping away from the body so I can go to her. I don't know if she can hear me, but her eyes look alert, so I have to assume she knows what's going on. "It'll be okay. I know I've scared you, baby, but I swear, I would never hurt you. I'll never let anything hurt you. I swear it."

My chest aches. I need her to believe that.

What if everything's changed now? What if this one night ruined us forever?

My cellphone is still in the car, and like hell I'm going to leave this room, even with all my enemies incapacitated. I grab Casey's cell phone and dial Luc's number.

I don't even wait for him to greet me. "Get here now," I tell him. "Bring clean up. I have him." Then I hang up. That's all he really needs to hear, anyway.

I toss the phone aside, then move over towards Alexander. His mouth is slack and his breaths are incredibly shallow. He's on death's door, I think grimly, although I'm not stupid enough to think that something like this could genuinely take him out.

No, he's going to live. He's going to live, and I'm going to deliver him to Luc, and I'm going to get exactly what I want.

And it'll be worth nothing if Casey is too terrified to ever want me again.

I roll Alexander onto his stomach. Not a good position for a man struggling to breathe, but I couldn't give less of a fuck. I hope he's in incredible pain. Then I restrain his wrists with my belt. Perhaps not the most effective method, but it'll buy me a moment if he manages to miraculously recover enough to try to scramble away.

There. Now he's Luc's problem, and I can turn my attention to what actually matters.

Casey is frozen solid with the knife held out in front of her. I try to gently take the knife from her, really not wanting to end this night with either of us getting stabbed. I'm sure she's furious and freaked out enough to want to stab me, and honestly, I'd probably let her have a free go at it, but I know her. She'd feel guilty about it later.

I brush her hand by accident when attempting to grasp the knife handle, and she comes back to alertness, life breathed back into her limbs. She immediately grips the knife tighter.

"Casey? Baby? Can I take this? I don't want you to hurt yourself," I say as soothingly as I can manage.

"What the fuck just happened, Max?" she whispers, eyes darting around the room like she's going to see something that makes this all make sense to her. But I know what she's seeing. Blood, two corpses, a man who is very close to being a corpse, and her family, still frozen.

I sigh, squaring my shoulders. When I envisioned having this conversation, I always imagined we'd be calm. Sitting together in the living room, maybe. And I'd get to hold her hand and explain it slowly. I'd transform for her to see, but I'd show her a big, loveable puppy dog she could pet and love on, letting her touch me in a way no one else ever has. I'd be able to turn back once I convinced her and lay out all our options, because I'd be able to offer her eternity at my side if she wanted it.

But instead, I scared her shitless today. I ripped out throats and broke necks in front of her. I realize belatedly that I'm standing in front of her naked and covered in blood.

But I have to tell her. And I have to hope I can convince her I'm still worth being with.

It'll kill me if she leaves me. I won't force her to stay, of course, and I won't guilt her by telling her, but it will kill me. I might be able to convince myself to keep going forward so I can be her guardian angel from the shadows, but I can't think of a single other reason to keep living if she's not in my life anymore.

"When I was an infant, that man over there cursed me and Luc and others like us to be what you saw today," I tell her. "Wolves. Shifters. He trained us to fight."

"You're a werewolf?" she nearly shouts, her voice strangled with her disbelief.

"Yeah, baby. I am. Luc is too," I tell her, because I'm not going to hold anything back. "And we escaped Alexander—that's the guy tied up over there—and have been living our lives. Everything else you know about my life is true. Mostly," I correct hastily.

"What does mostly mean?" she demands. I can't help but notice that she's still holding the knife, even if her grip has slackened.

I shift my eyes. "Can we... away from..." I jerk my chin to Alexander and her family. I don't want to spill my heart to them. That is just for Casey.

She hesitates a second, and it makes my heart ache. Fuck, if she's scared of me, if I managed to make her scared—

I'll rip my own heart out and hand it to her before I make her afraid again. I need to convince her that I might be a scary dog, but she's always going to hold the leash.

She nods, and it doesn't escape my notice that the knife remains in her hand as she turns and walks towards the kitchen.

"What does mostly mean?" she asks again, turning back around to face me. I stop in my tracks with enough room between us to park a small car.

I hesitate, but I owe her the complete truth. "I'm two thousand years old, give or take," I tell her. "I'm not some politician. I'm a soldier and that's all I'll ever be. I'm Luc's enforcer for things like us, so they don't step out of line. Anything I might have ever told you about my childhood was bullshit."

She tilts her head. "And that's it?"

I nod. "That's it, baby. I know that's a lot, but I did everything I could to tell as few lies as possible. I swear."

"And the... animal?" she asks, clearly hesitant about calling me what I am.

"I turn into a wolf. My senses are sharper. I'm faster, stronger." I'm a lethal, violent predator, but that's more training than anything.

She nods again, and I wait with bated breath while she absorbs the information. She sets the knife down.

"What am I, Max?" she asks, and her voice is now quiet, the fight leaving. "What am I to you?"

My heart seizes. "You are the love of my life," I say quietly. "You are the only one that's made me feel like a person in two goddamn millennia. You are my reason for living, Casey. I swear. That hasn't changed, and it never fucking will."

"You didn't tell me," she whispers. "Was I just some..." She shakes her head. "I don't know. I just thought this was real. That we had everything."

Fuck this. I take a cautious step closer, and when she doesn't react, I keep moving until I could touch her if I reached out. "We do have everything, baby. I swear, I always intended to tell you. When I think of forever, you're it."

"You're two thousand years old," she says, incredulity clear in her voice.

"Yeah. And trust me, you've made every moment of that waiting worth it." And the torture, and the pain, and the death, and all the long, boring years in between. Every bit of it is worth it to be here with her. "I always wanted to tell you, Casey."

She crosses her arms and turns her head slightly. "You've had plenty of chances. I've told you everything, Max."

"I didn't want to tell you and have it just be something that could come between us. I made a deal with Luc, sweetheart, that he'd do everything in his power to find me a way to make you immortal like me, or a way for me to be mortal like you. You know, if you want that."

She's absolutely silent for a minute, and I dare to look her over. I didn't even check her for injuries earlier. She's covered in blood, but I know without asking that none of it is hers, at least.

Fuck, I killed people in front of her. I stained her house, the safe place we built together, in blood. I wouldn't be surprised if she said no, that she wants nothing to do with me anymore.

"So, what now?" she asks, her voice oddly empty. "I can guess it could be hard to really plan for a forever, when you're going to outlive me by so long."

Fuck that. I won't outlive her by a single moment. Whether or not she eventually accepts my offer for immortality is immaterial.

"That guy in there?" I say, jerking my thumb carelessly over my shoulder. "He's the one who made me like this. Luc gave me the lead on how to find him, because if he can make me and Luc and probably hundreds of others, we can probably make you immortal." I hesitate a moment, hating to say it, but needing her to know she has options. "If you want that, of course."

She doesn't say anything for a long moment. I should give her space and let her process the astronomical amount of information I just dumped on her, but I get the irrational fear that, if I leave this room, I'll never see her again. I have this one chance to make her understand. I never wanted to have to tell her like this, but this is the hand I've been dealt, and I need to show her that there are upsides to this life.

"Baby," I say, and I know I'm begging, but I couldn't care less. "I'm so fucking sorry you saw the absolute worst of my world tonight. I never wanted you to see that." I swallow, because here's the hard truth. "I never wanted you to see me like that. I am that man. I'm a monster in the dark and I won't lie and pretend that's the first time I've ever killed someone.

It's not. I couldn't even give a guess at how many I've killed. I'm not a good man, and I'm sorry you had to find out like this, but I am yours. I'll do bad things for you, and I swear on my life, I'll never, ever hurt you."

"I know that." Her voice is still too-soft, a little dazed, but cold relief washes through me to hear that even right now she knows that I'd never hurt her.

I half want to tell her about the power she wields, wanting to explain exactly how much I scare people and exactly how much I'm willing and eager to do whatever she asks me to do. That she has a leash on this werewolf, and I'll happily rip out throats for her and then return for fucking belly rubs.

I don't think she's quite ready to hear that part yet. But we'll get there.

Only if she accepts me back, I realize. She hasn't said anything else.

"Sweetheart, absolutely no pressure, and I'm sorry to ask anything of you right now," I begin slowly, softly, trying not to startle her. "But I kind of need to know what you're thinking."

"You ruined the Christmas party," she blurts out, then claps her hand over her mouth, her eyes going wide with shock.

But I have to suppress a grin. Because if she's worried about shit like that, then she's not going to throw me out. "You're right," I agree, then cross the last of the distance between us and sink to my knees in front of her. I take the hand not over her mouth in both of mine, rubbing gently at it, just needing to hold some part of her. "Tell me how to make it up to you."

She takes the hand off her mouth and I grab it before she can cover her face again. "I didn't mean that," she says, words spilling out too fast now. "That was a stupid thing to say, sorry, I just said the first thing on my mind—"

"I did ruin your Christmas party," I interrupt her gently. "Tell me how to make it up to you."

She tries to pull her hands from mine fruitlessly. I keep rubbing her hands as gently as I can while also not letting her run from me.

"I watched someone try to kill you in front of me," she whispers, some shock creeping back into her voice. "And then I—you don't need to make anything up to me, Max."

She's worried because someone tried to kill me? I make a mental note to wait a bit before I explain exactly why I was late getting home today. She's so fucking cute to be worried about me like this.

"Sweetheart, I hate to be the one to tell you this, but they tried to kill you, too," I say as gently as I can.

"I'm aware." She winces. "Me stabbing him just made it worse, didn't it?"

It probably didn't change anything, because it's not like he was going to leave her alone before that. "It was fucking hot," I tell her instead of explaining. "Like, really fucking hot." A total understatement, but I feel like we have a little more to get through before I can explain that it made me want to fuck her until we both fall into an exhausted heap on the floor.

"Get up, Max," she says quietly, squeezing my hands.

But I just shake my head, because I'm not done yet. "I'm sorry I ruined your Christmas party," I tell her. "And that I brought danger into your home, and violence. And that I probably scared you tonight."

"You didn't scare me," she says firmly. "You could never—I trust you with everything, Max."

My heart beats even faster. "You can trust me, baby," I promise her. "I'll always put you first." Then, instead of getting up like she wants, I lean forward, resting my head on her soft belly, dropping her hands so I can carefully wrap my arms around her thighs, holding her to me.

"I'm sorry I kept this from you," I tell her, words pressed against that sweater dress, which is now blood-splattered and not as soft as it looked earlier. "I'm so sorry, sweetheart."

Her hand runs through my hair, and I close my eyes, at peace for the first time all night. Maybe for the first time in my life, honestly. This is us, completely honest with each other, and she's still here.

"Don't lie to me again," she whispers.

"I won't. I fucking promise, Casey. There's nothing left I haven't told you. It's just us forever."

Footsteps behind us break me out of my stupor, but I can smell who it is quick enough to settle me, so I don't bother moving.

Luc walks into the kitchen. He raises an eyebrow at the sight of me on my knees, but he doesn't comment. "You leave your house defenseless like this?" he asks, clearly having just walked through our broken down front door.

I move to stand reluctantly, and he looks me over again. "You always greet your guests naked?"

Fucker. Not like he hasn't seen it before.

I move to stand in front of Casey, absolutely sure that she's had enough of people barging into her home tonight, but her hand wraps around my bicep, and I wonder if she can't stand the separation any more than I can.

Luc notices. "Ms. Jackson."

She swallows, and her hand briefly tightens on my arm. "Governor Lawson."

He gives a cold half-smile. "I think, given the circumstances, you should probably call me Luc."

"Given that you're in my house to help clean up some bodies, you should probably call me Casey."

"Alright, Casey. How are you handling tonight?" he asks, sounding more genuinely caring than anything I've heard from him in a while.

She takes a shaky breath. "Adjusting. How do we handle this?"

He nods crisply. "Several of our associates are waiting outside. They can handle the bodies. As for Alexander, you have no idea how long I've been waiting to get my hands on him."

There's an almost manic gleam in his eyes, hidden behind his calm exterior. You'd have to know him to see it, but I've had too much practice reading Luc. If it were anyone but Alexander, I'd pity the night he's about to have.

"You owe me answers," I remind him.

"You'll be the first to hear," he promises.

I watch him for a minute. I've never questioned him, never pushed, but this time, I have to know. And considering it's Alexander, our childhood bogeyman, lying unconscious out there, I take a chance. "What do you want with him, Luc? For real. You didn't go to all this effort for my sake."

He tilts his head. "No, but you were convenient bait."

"Bait?" The word comes out as barely more than a growl. Casey squeezes my arm again, but Luc doesn't even blink.

"You always interested him. The perfect soldier who turned away from him. If I could use you to draw him closer, we both got what we wanted." He looks over at Casey like he can see her through my body and actually winces. "I am sorry you got dragged in, though, Casey. I try to keep humans out of our business."

"Except when you're running against them for office," she retorts, and my heart squeezes. Brave girl.

He smiles. "Yes, except for then."

"You haven't answered my question," I interrupt. "What do you want him for?"

Luc looks at me for a long moment, unblinking. "You're not the only one of us who found someone, Max," is all he says before turning fully away from us. He turns to talk over his shoulder. "Go get cleaned up. I'm assuming the others will wake up when we remove Alexander. Don't want them to see you naked, Max."

"Don't touch them," I say automatically, my mind still spinning over what he said.

Cold Luc has found someone? Surely he's talking about another one of the shifters he's gathered over the years.

"Go get dressed."

Casey squeezes my arm again, and I turn, scooping her up into my arms to carry her upstairs.

When I set her down, she's getting close to hyperventilating. "I can't," she says, and I immediately scoop her back up to squeeze her tight, trying to ground her. "I forgot they were here and I can't do it, I can't face my family and explain what just happened."

I squeeze a little tighter, marveling at how this is somehow the straw that breaks the camel's back. "You don't have to," I murmur. "We're going to make sure they don't remember anything, don't worry about that."

"I can't," she insists anyway. "I can't face them, not after—there are bloodstains in our house, Max, and I just saw... I can't."

"You don't have to," I say again. "Baby, you don't have to do anything. Especially not with those assholes. You're not obligated to entertain them. We can try again some other night. Or never. Either option works for me."

I'm personally voting for never, but I don't say it out loud to her. I haven't forgotten how they spoke to her, nor will I ever.

It takes her a few minutes to regulate her breathing, but she has no more arguments. "I want them gone," she says eventually, her voice more level now.

"Then they'll be gone. This is your home," I emphasize.

She nods shakily. "I'm ready to get changed. Sorry."

"Don't be sorry, sweetheart." I look her up and down as I step back, frowning. "You should bring your clothes downstairs. Luc's boys can dispose of them, hide the blood."

"Oh," she murmurs, and I wince, but she just starts stripping mechanically, so I turn to my dresser.

I groan when I turn back and get a view of her, sweatpants in my hand. "Baby, were you wearing that for me?"

Is she supposed to be a sexy Santa with all that red? Fuck me, I never thought I'd think sexy Santa, but apparently that's

128

a concept I'm more than on board with. There's a little red bow right in the middle of her bra, and I'm damned tempted to tell Luc to take care of everything and unwrap her like a present.

"It was supposed to be for later," she mutters.

I drop my sweatpants and move to her, running a hand over her hip. "I can act surprised later." It's a bold thing to say, assuming I'll get lucky tonight. I hold my breath.

She actually manages to giggle a bit, and getting her to react that way loosens something in my chest. We're going to be okay. "I'd appreciate that, Max."

I kiss the top of her head. "I'll be surprised, and I'll tell you how fucking sexy you are, how you are the hottest thing I've ever seen, how—"

There's a thump from downstairs, no doubt a body being moved. Casey flinches and turns, only settling when I rub firmly over her hip again.

"Save that thought," I tell her, turning away so I can pull on my sweatpants.

December 24th, 8:30 pm

When we emerge downstairs, the bodies are gone, three men are frantically scrubbing at the bloodstains, and Luc stands over Alexander as if just daring him to wake up and face him.

He looks over at me, wearing just sweatpants, not even bothering with a shirt, and raises an eyebrow. I expect a snide comment, but all he says is, "Are you ready?"

"They been dosed?" Casey squeezes my hand at the question, but I just squeeze back. I'll explain in a minute.

"No, we left that to you. Wasn't sure how much you wanted to tell your in-laws."

I want to never talk to them again, but I don't say that. Not when Casey is so fragile about them right now. Instead, I nod. "Alright. Casey, baby, any way you could make some tea?"

"Tea?" she asks, voice high and a little incredulous. When I just nod and turn towards the kitchen, she frowns, following me. "Why tea, Max?"

I go to the cabinet over the fridge, the one Casey wouldn't have a hope of reaching unless she climbed onto the counter, and fish all the way in the back, pulling out a silver aerosol canister. "This is why," I explain. "A witch showed us how to make this a few centuries ago." In exchange for her life, although I don't mention that part to Casey. "It helps mortals forget. In the air it will make them confused. Consumed in, say, tea, it will make the last few hours a fuzzy, blank place in their minds. They won't worry about the absence; they sort of just develop a neutral feeling about the time, not needing to explore it any further."

Casey goes entirely still. "It's in our house," she whispers.

I nod. "Most of us keep some, just in case."

"Have you ever used it on me?"

Fucking hell. I rush forward, already shaking my head. "No, Casey, sweetheart. I swear. That was never... I never would. I haven't touched your mind. If you had found out earlier, I would have done the same thing I did today. I swear."

She looks at me for a long moment, staring into my soul. I make myself hold her gaze, needing her to see my honesty. At last, she nods.

"Any type of tea?"

"Hot liquid makes it taste better, but anything would work," I confirm, holding my breath as she turns away, but she seems over her fear.

"And they'll really just forget? All of this?"

131

"I hope they don't forget you telling them off earlier," I say, taking a moment to relish the memory. "But if they do, I have no problem re-enacting it later. Make sure they got the point and all."

She laughs a little again, and my shoulders relax. It's a little broken, but under the circumstances, it's definitely more than I hoped for.

While we wait for the kettle to boil, I slide behind her, running my hand underneath the hem of my sweatshirt that she's wearing, stroking over her belly and hips. "Tell me what you're thinking," I whisper, needing a way into her brain.

"I'm thinking that this is insane. That this is some weird, stress-induced dream and I'm going to wake up and demand you hug me for like twelve hours so I can recover."

"Not a dream," I tell her. "I can still hold you for twelve hours. Or longer." I hesitate a moment. "Is it that bad?"

She's silent for a long moment. "Is it always this much?"

"No, sweetheart. I promise. This is a lot, I know. But usually, you won't ever know the difference." I grin, even if she can't see it. "Hell, you might just forget that I'm a big wolf underneath this."

"Unless I also become a werewolf." Her words are deceptively casual, but my whole body freezes.

I take a few deep breaths, using her scent to calm me down. Fuck, we're really doing this, talk about our future, talk about forever.

I do my best to match her casual tone, though. I don't want to scare her away from this. "Technically, we don't know what type of animal you'd be. We don't know how Alexander's spell works, either. But we've found an entire fucking zoo's worth of different animals." I'm about to ask her if she's serious, if she's considering it, when the kettle boils.

"Let's do this," she murmurs, pouring the water into the teapot with little stars I got her last Christmas.

I hold still for a moment, but then drop my hands from her. Probably better to discuss this when we don't have an audience in the next room. I turn to get mugs and bite my tongue.

When I've deposited the mugs on the counter and a kiss to Casey's head, I reluctantly leave her for a minute to go talk to Luc.

"How'd it go?" he asks me quietly, not turning to look at me, keeping his eyes trained on Alexander.

"About as well as I could expect, considering," I tell him. "I'm going to dose them."

He nods. "Once the tea is ready, I'll pull him out of here. I already told the others to get lost. Your house isn't exactly clean, but..."

But nothing short of some crime scene specialists will do that, and we're not exactly about to report this incident. I add planning for a remodel or a move to my to-do list.

I walk over to Casey's family, making myself look each of them in their terrified eyes. "You won't remember this," I say quietly, despite the fact that Luc can certainly hear me. "But maybe the idea will stick around in your brains. Casey is too good for all of you. And next time she calls, she deserves a loving family and some fucking gratitude." When I finish, I open the canister. Some genius thought it'd be a bright idea for us to store this in pepper spray canisters, and I take perverse pleasure in giving each of them a squirt in the face.

It settles like a thin mist, making their faces slightly damp. There's no outward change, and they don't become alert, but I know it's working. As soon as they breathed it in, they started to forget.

Fuck. Casey. "Casey, baby, don't come in here for a minute," I call. That should give it enough time to dissipate.

"Tea's not done yet," she calls back.

There's movement behind me, and I turn to see Alexander twitching lightly. Luc stomps on his neck, then turns to me, an unimpressed eyebrow raised. "Subpar work," he criticizes.

"Fuck you. I had other things on my mind." Like the man trying to kill my wife.

He shrugs. "No excuse for sloppy work." He turns his attention to Alexander. "Don't worry, though. There's plenty more where that came from, and I'm just getting started."

After two minutes, I hear shuffling in the kitchen. "Can I come in now?"

"That's my cue," Luc says, bending over to heft Alexander's deadweight frame over his scrawny shoulder. It should look ridiculous, but Luc carries the burden with ease. "We'll talk soon."

I nod, done with him, and move towards Casey. "I'll take those. Give it another two minutes," I advise, taking the tray of mugs from her and setting it on the dining room table.

Her family starts to wake up, the spell wearing off, just as I finish pouring a few drops into each of their mugs. They look around, blinking in confusion.

"Casey says tea's ready," I tell them, like we're picking up mid-conversation, and deposit a mug in front of them. They're so disoriented that they sip almost on instinct, and Casey's mom doesn't even comment on the very plebeian mugs I've offered them.

All it takes is one sip. Their eyes, already disoriented, become completely blank for a long moment, and I know we've taken tonight from them.

It's better for humans. That's why we carry this mixture in the first place; most humans can't handle peeks at our world. It takes a special human like Casey to accept it, and she's one of a kind.

She walks into the dining room after a moment, no doubt exactly when two minutes are up. I give her a small nod, and she nods back, face set. Determined.

"Thank you for coming tonight," I tell them. "It was great to meet you all." Sometimes small lies are necessary, I suppose. "I don't want you to be here too late; after all, tomorrow is an important day."

Casey's father would have a conniption if someone talked to him that way normally, I know, but now he just nods and stands.

They don't say anything as they leave, and I wrap an arm around Casey's waist, holding her to my side as we watch out of our wrecked front door as they move to their cars.

"Are they okay to drive?" Casey murmurs.

"Should be. It blurs their recent memories, but not their skills or their senses."

She looks around her. "How are we supposed to sleep in a house with no door tonight?"

I kiss her head. "We can go somewhere else if you'll feel better," I offer.

"On Christmas Eve?"

Fair point. I'm not super eager to have our own no room at the inn moment. "I swear, baby. I'm the scariest thing out there. And I'll keep you safe." I let her go long enough to find the door that was kicked off the hinges and prop it in place, closing us on the inside. It won't be secure, and if someone looks for more than a moment, it'll be evident that something is wrong, but it's at least something.

It's like closing the door shuts out the outside world completely. I can see Casey visibly relax, like all the tension is just gone. Her parents, Luc, Alexander, the entire world and the secret of what I am—it's gone. It's just us again, in our home that is our sanctuary.

Of course, that'll disappear as soon as she sees the first bloodstain in our dining room, so I try to steer her back to the kitchen, but she shakes me off. "Need to clean up," she murmurs.

"Baby, the blood is going to take a whole remodel. We're not getting it out tonight."

"The food, Max," she says. "The dishes. Dinner."

I hesitate, not wanting her to have to do any work after the shitshow we just went through, but nod. "I'll clear if you start washing," I bargain, not wanting her in the room where she watched people die.

She hesitates, but gives in with a nod, turning to the kitchen.

We work in silence for a while, until she turns off the water and joins me in drying dishes. "There's one more thing that we didn't talk about," she tells me.

"Oh yeah?" I ask, frantically scanning my brain for what I could have missed.

"You called me your wife earlier."

"I always call you my wife," I tell her immediately. "I just didn't say it out loud until I could make til death do us part not sound like such a fucking joke." I hold my breath. I know she wants to get married, and I know she sees us as having that sort of future. I know it's been me holding us back, but that doesn't mean she still wants that after today.

She turns back to her dishrag. "I want tattooed wedding bands," she says simply, not looking at me, just leaving that out there.

Fuck. Yes. My heart might actually stop beating for a moment, the joy practically killing me for a second.

"Yes," I say, ignoring how hoarse my voice sounds. "Fuck, yes, Casey. Yes. A thousand times yes."

"You have to get one too."

"In a fucking heartbeat. I know someone who does tattoos for people like me."

She looks up at that, mouth half open, no doubt to ask about how tattoos work for me. But right now, I really don't have the brainpower to explain tattoos.

I throw down my towel for drying dishes and take hers from her hand, tossing it on the counter. I couldn't give less of a fuck about the dishes. They'll be here tomorrow, and Casey just told me she'll marry me.

"We were interrupted earlier," I murmur, stepping up behind her and pulling her flush to me, then running my hands up under the sweatshirt she's wearing. I groan when

138

my hands reach that taunting little bow at the center of her bra. "Fuck me, baby. My wife is so fucking perfect."

She giggles. "I'm not your wife yet."

"Fuck that. You're my wife in every way that matters." I pause for a second, considering. "Want to get married tomorrow?" I think it's too late tonight to rush out and get married, but if she thinks we could pull it off, I'd go right now.

"Tomorrow is Christmas, Max."

"So?" I kiss up the side of her neck, pushing her curls out of the way with my nose so I can reach more skin.

"So, good luck getting a marriage license."

"Luc's the governor," I argue. Shit, can I get Luc to marry us? I spend half a second daydreaming about the look on his face if I ever asked him that. "Do you want a big wedding?" I can't picture it, her with a crowd of eyes watching us, or a finicky little ceremony where everything has to be just so, or the big white dress. But if she wants it, then it's hers.

She snorts. "Fuck no." She turns in my arms, her arms wrapping around my neck, holding me to her like I'd ever even think about going. "Just you and me, some officiant and whoever we need to witness it. You're all I need."

"You're all I need too, baby," I say, although at this point I'm pretty sure that's a foregone conclusion. I stroke my hands over her ribs, teasing at the bottom of her breasts. "You're everything, Casey." I lean down and kiss her, unable to resist it even a moment longer. "But, soon?" I ask when I pull back, leaning our foreheads together.

She laughs slightly, playing with the ends of my hair and making me melt. "You've waited all this time, what's a while longer?"

"I want to be your husband, baby," I say, and, tired of having any amount of space between us, I pick her up. She automatically wraps her legs around my hips, latching on. "I want to be your husband so damned bad. I promise I'll be a good husband."

Her eyes go soft. "I know you will be. Soon," she promises. "Not tomorrow. But soon."

Tomorrow I can focus on convincing her that soon should mean as soon as possible. For tonight, I just want to show her that I can be the best damn husband.

"Soon," I agree, hands trailing up under her sweatshirt again. Fuck me, I don't think I've ever been so desperate for her. I could drown in her right now, looking up into those brown eyes as I hitch her higher against me.

She grinds her cunt against me, and I can't help but groan. "I guess this explains why you can carry me around so easily," she muses, still annoyingly rational, even as all my blood has long since left my brain.

Right. I used to make up elaborate gym routines to explain my strength to her. "Does this mean you'll allow me to carry you more often?" I grab her waist a little tighter, helping her rock against me for a moment before I push the sweatshirt up.

She takes it off for me, discarding it on the kitchen floor, and that red bra with the red bow is even better the second time around. Her tits are spilling out of it, a present for me to unwrap. I can see the outline of her nipple through the nearly transparent lace, and I want that in my mouth enough that I can feel myself drooling for it.

"We'll see," she says, now running her hands through my hair.

"Can I take you upstairs?" I'm already moving before she answers, not even looking as I carry her upstairs. I'm too lost in her eyes, in the feel of her soft skin under my hands, in the way she touches me back.

I shove our bedroom door shut with my foot, moving to lay her out on the bed before stepping back. "You're so fucking beautiful."

She wiggles off her sweatpants in response, and I move to help her, tugging them down to reveal miles of soft, inked skin and those pretty red panties.

She kicks her pants onto the floor, and I trace the band of the panties over her hip. "It's almost a shame these are so god-damn pretty," I tell her, sliding my finger under the material. "'Cause I'm two seconds from ripping them off you."

"Do you have any idea how much these cost?" she asks, but she doesn't sound upset. In fact, I watch hungrily as she spreads her thighs for me, giving me a perfect view.

I slide down to my knees, gently tugging her further to the edge of the bed so I can place her thighs over my shoulders and bring my face level with her cunt. I lean in, running my nose along the seam of the fabric. "You smell fucking perfect," I murmur, turning my head and pressing a kiss against that crescent moon tattoo on her thigh I love so damned much. Then, I return to her lace-covered cunt, teasing with my tongue before I find her clit, doing my best to suck through the fabric.

She lets out a toe-curling groan and tightens her thighs on my head. "That's it, baby," I murmur. "Show your husband how well he pleasures you."

"My husband is a tease," she complains, but she's still squeezing my head, so I just smile.

"Have you ever known your husband to not follow through?" Before she can answer, I tug the panties, tearing them at her left hip and throwing the fabric somewhere behind me.

If she plans to scold me, it gets lost in her moans when I immediately suck her clit between my lips. She tastes so fucking sweet, already wet and soft for me, and I have to reach down to adjust my cock.

She makes me so fucking hard. She ruins me completely, endlessly, and I want nothing more than to be ruined by her forever. To let her lay claim to my body, my heart, my mind. I'm hers.

"Ma-ax," she whines, a high-pitched noise that drags my name into multiple syllables.

I pull back. "Yeah, baby?"

"I want you inside me. Please." Her hands grab for my hair, completely contradicting what she's saying as she holds me in place and tries to grind against my face.

I smile. Good fucking girl, chasing her pleasure. Like I could feel her little fingers steering me like that and ever move from where I am. "Come on my face first, sweetheart. I need to be dripping with your come. I need to be able to taste only you for the rest of the night." I lean forward to run my nose through her folds. "Give me what I need, and let your husband give you what you need. Ride my face, baby."

She groans, and her fingers tighten in my hair as I settle back in, torn between wanting this to last forever and wanting her to come all over me as fast as possible.

Her little moans and her hips bucking against my face decide for me. I palm my cock through my sweats with one hand, then use my other hand to push two fingers inside her, curving them to make her scream.

She doesn't disappoint, arching her hips towards my face and shouting my name, squeezing my head with her thighs.

I have her close now, and all I can think about is making her come.

When she goes over that edge, she squeezes my head so hard I don't think I'm ever going to move again, and I slurp at her cunt, desperate for the taste of her, soaking in her scent.

Casey pushes me away, releasing my head and using a hand to weakly shove at me. I take the hint and pull back, admiring her tits heaving and still spilling out of that red bra.

She looks down at me, smiling weakly. "What a good husband, Max."

And that makes me absolutely feral. I snarl, pushing to my feet so I can push her back into the bed, laying on top of her, needing to feel every inch of her against me. I kiss her, making her taste herself on my tongue. She groans and grabs at my shoulders, then lets her hands trail down until she's pushing at my sweatpants.

I stand up enough to kick the pants off, needing to be closer to her, needing to not have an inch of space between us. My fucking wife, all splayed out on our bed, eyes heavy from coming and looking so damn ready to fuck.

"What do you want, baby?" I ask, crawling back onto the bed. "Tell me how I can make you happy."

She considers for a moment. "I want to ride you."

"Fuck yes," I say, the words ripped out of me as I scramble to sit up on the edge of the bed, spreading my thighs enough so she'll have a place to sit. "Going to use my cock to make yourself come, sweetheart?"

She smiles as she sits up, moving to straddle me. "Going to watch that look you get in your eyes when we're fucking."

I nip at the top of her breast. "What look, baby?"

She winds her arms around my neck. "Like you can't believe it. Like it's genuinely the best thing that's ever happened to you."

"That's because it absolutely is," I agree, then groan as she sinks down on my cock with absolutely no warning. "Fuck, sweetheart. Go slow."

"No," she says, rocking her hips to somehow take even more of me. I'm so deep in her, and she's absolutely squeezing around me. I'm going to come in a minute flat if she doesn't slow down.

"Baby." I'm absolutely begging her not to push me over the edge so quickly.

She tilts my face up and kisses me, slow and sweet. She has a soft smile when she pulls away. "Let your wife take care of you, Max."

Fucking hell.

She rides me with slow, gentle rocks of her hips. To distract myself, I flick the back of that pretty red bra open and let it fall down her shoulders until she unwinds her arms from my neck to toss it aside.

Her tits are devastatingly beautiful when she rides me, and I should have known that this would be a very ineffectual distraction.

I bury my face between them, trying to hide my groan against her skin.

She chuckles and strokes her fingers through my hair, lighting every nerve in my head on fire. How is my scalp a fucking erogenous zone? Somehow, Casey makes it one.

"C'mon, baby," she murmurs, and then rides me in earnest.

It's all I can do to get my hands around her waist to support her and hang on as her perfect fucking cunt works around my cock. I suck her nipple into my mouth, earning a groan and her fingernails briefly digging into my scalp for my trouble. "Max," she murmurs, voice breathy. Her cunt is fluttering in a way that tells me she's close. "Look at me, please."

I release her nipple and look at her, finding her staring right back in such a soft, tender way that I could just fall apart. This isn't fucking like we've ever done it before, I suddenly realize. We can say whatever vows we want in front of whoever we need to in the future. This, right here—this is our bond. Our promise.

She knows it too. I can see it in her eyes.

"You're mine," I whisper to her, in absolute awe as I watch her. "You're mine forever."

"And you're mine," she agrees, the sentence ending in a cute little moan. "God, Max—I'm so damn close."

"I know you are," I soothe, rubbing my hands up her side, palming the underside of her breasts before slipping them back down. "Come for me, Casey. Come all over my cock. Mark me as yours."

I can see it in her eyes first, that hazy pleasure that completely overtakes her. And then I feel her squeeze around me before she collapses against me, coming hard enough her body jerks.

"My good fucking girl," I murmur to her, bucking my hips erratically as I hold her through it. "My perfect fucking wife. So damn good for me."

She moans and tries to circle her hips, which I take as my sign. Grabbing her hips, I rock her onto my cock, thrusting against her as much as I'm capable of until my orgasm sweeps over me, pulsing through my body and making me almost black out with pleasure.

She's peppering kisses over my face when I feel like I can open my eyes again, and I steal a long, heated kiss when she gets too close to my lips. By the time I pull back, she's wiggling slightly, so I pull out before she gets too sensitive.

She's dripping come and I can't suppress a groan, unable to resist reaching down to gently push some of it back inside.

"Caveman," she accuses with absolutely no heat.

"Consummating my marriage with my wife," I counter, pushing more of my come back inside her. I leave her swollen, slick cunt alone so I can grab her hips and remove her from my lap, laying her down on the bed so she can rest. It also affords me a great view of her.

Fuck, this woman is mine. This woman is so mine that she's agreed to stick with me for literal eternity. Til death do us part, forever and ever, amen. She is mine.

And I'm hers. I've been hers since the day we met. Since the day I first saw her, really. But now she really knows. Now she knows everything, and I—with my secrets and my past and my future—am hers.

"I should clean you up," I say, reluctant to move, but not wanting her to be uncomfortable.

Instead, she grabs my hand and tugs me until I willingly lie down next to her, my head on her chest. "In a minute. Don't pretend you're not loving the idea of your come inside me."

Yeah, okay. I am. Sue me. She looks fucking perfect like this.

She takes my hand and plays with my fingers, and I'm so fucked stupid that it takes me a long moment to realize she's playing with my left ring finger. "Soon?" I ask her.

"Soon," she agrees. "Is next week too soon?"

My fucking woman, on the same wavelength as me. "Baby, you could suggest an hour from now and I'd be all over it."

"That would require us to get dressed."

"Fair point." I settle in deeper, using her tits as a pillow, and allowing my eyes to drift closed as I rest in my own personal heaven.

"Unless you don't want to marry me until you're sure the immortality thing is real." She whispers it, doubt in her voice, and I need to erase that doubt immediately.

"I would marry you in any situation," I tell her, sitting up so I can see her, so she knows I'm serious. "I was stupid to wait. I would marry you, immortality or no immortality. I don't give a fuck. I'm yours for however long we have, and I want the world to know that." I pause for a beat. "But the immortality thing will happen soon. I've never known Luc to fail at something he sets his mind to." An understatement. I'm sure Alexander is already pleading for mercy, and I'm equally sure that Luc is a long way away from granting it. "We'll get that spell, baby. If you want it."

I can't demand she live with me forever. I can't make her take on this world. I hope she'll give me a chance to prove that it has positive elements, too, and won't make her decision just based on today, but I wouldn't blame her if she was put off.

She's quiet for a moment, but then asks, "What kind of animal do you think I'll be?"

I smile and lie down to rest my head on her chest again. I couldn't give less of a fuck what kind of animal she is, as long as she's mine and I'm hers. That's all that matters, now.

December 25th, 8:00 am

One Year Later

It's eight in the morning on Christmas, and we haven't managed to get out of bed.

We've managed to actually fuck ourselves out. One year, one wedding, one very expensive home remodel, and one life-changing spell later, we still can't keep our hands off each other.

But now we're well-satiated and just holding each other. There's a beautiful tree and a pile of presents downstairs, but all I want to do is play with her tattooed ring finger.

Her tattoo is a normal one, the very last silver-free tattoo she'll ever be able to get. She hasn't gotten a new tattoo since the spell, but she's watched me get three, and I think she'll probably be planning a new one soon.

The spell took two months to set up after Luc beat it out of Alexander. I haven't asked what Luc did with him. I'm relatively sure he's still alive, and also positive that he's very much wishing he wasn't.

Casey turns her head, kissing the tattoos on my chest. I have a wedding band on my left hand too, but I got two others now that I could get tattoos without offending Casey that we didn't get them together.

Her name is stenciled over my heart in her own handwriting. Beneath that is the paw print of her wolf form.

She's a fucking pretty wolf, all reddish-brown fur and big brown eyes with a playful glint. I've never thought of the wolf form as something playful before, but Casey brings it out in me every day now.

I'm still that scary fucker that Luc needs me to be. That guy is never going away. But with her, with my wife, I can just be. Be playful, relaxed, and happy.

So goddamn happy. Happier than I ever knew a person could be.

I kiss the top of her head, pressing my face into her curls for a deep draw of her sweet scent. Then I raise her ring finger to my mouth, kissing it gently.

"Time for Christmas?" she asks.

"Am I going to find you under my Christmas tree?"

"You might find something you could re-wrap me in under the Christmas tree," she offers.

I'm up in a flash, then scoop her up into my arms, bridal carrying her out of our room and down the stairs, both of us still naked and her laughing the entire way.

Looking for more?

Receive two bonus scenes about Max and Casey when you sign up for my newsletter at www.addyjameswriter.com!

A Recipe for Love Sneak Peak

Looking for more? Meet Marcus and Elise next! The immortal, reclusive dragon is starting over his life once again—but he never expected to fall in love with a chef!

Book Tropes include:

*Dragon shifter

*Billionaire/personal chef

*Fated mates

*Touch her and die

*Gift giving/spoiling

*He helps her heal

The conversation is tedious beyond belief. At least the wine is passable, and I sip at it as I stare around the ballroom rented for tonight's event.

This place is a who's-who of New York's old money crowds, and I should probably try harder to make connections. My new identity needs people to make him seem more legitimate, and as I take over my own company yet again, I should really have a network of the New York elite behind me.

I know all this, but it's tedious and I've done it too many times before. I check my watch, trying to calculate exactly how long I need to stay here before it's only mildly offensive for me to leave.

And all thoughts leave my head when I taste the appetizer.

Saganaki is something I've had before, having traveled to Greece multiple times. It's not that the dish is new or especially exciting for me. Still, something about it draws me in.

It's just right. Perfectly made with a delicate touch, and it captures my attention in a way nothing else has lately.

I flag down the nearest server. "I want to speak with the chef."

The poor man looks instantly terrified, but runs off before I can add that I want to say positive things to the chef. Shit. If he scares off whoever made this meal, if I managed to scare him that badly...

I need to control myself. Dragons tend to terrify humans, triggering long-dormant prey instincts still buried somewhere in their brains, and it takes careful control to avoid scaring the humans. It's not unusual for me to accidentally make a human feel what they perceive as an unexplained but deep sense of fear just by one look in my eyes.

Still, something tells me that this is important. That I can't afford to mess this up in any way, and if the server is too scared to get me the chef, then it will be a tragedy for us all.

A harried chef approaches my table. She's tall, thin, and her light hair is contained in a tight knot. "I was told you wanted to speak to me?"

I frown, looking her over. I still have the undeniable urge to speak to the chef, but this woman doesn't make me feel anything in particular.

"You made the appetizers?"

She straightens. "I'm the head chef here tonight; everything that comes from the kitchen went through me."

I eye her for a moment. She's protective, I think, and that's a trait I can admire well enough. "I wanted to say how good it was."

"Oh." She deflates slightly, defensive posturing dropped when she realizes that I'm not a threat to her staff. "Elise made them. I'll pass on your compliments."

"I'd like to meet Elise."

She stares at me, clearly trying to take my measure. I just look back, trying to keep my expression neutral. "Alright," she says at last. "Give me a moment, then."

She goes back to the kitchen, and three minutes later another chef appears.

This time, my dragon's instincts respond. Yes, this is who I was looking for.

Elise speed-walks across the room towards me. I watch with rapt attention, trying to figure out why my dragon is so insistent on this human.

Yes, she makes good food, but I've known hundreds of humans who do that. She's attractive, too, with clear dark eyes and ample curves, but I didn't come to this party tonight to pick someone up.

I watch her as she gets closer, and I can't deny that she's exactly the type I'd pick up if I was looking. But she's working, and I'm just some rich guy attending a party. I can't ask her to come home with me. The power differential is too weird.

"Hi, I'm Elise. Lacey said you wanted to talk to me, sir?"

Shit, she's stopped in front of me now, brown eyes watching me intently, and I have yet to figure out exactly why I want her here so badly.

I know the rest of my table is staring, and I just tune them out. Maybe Marcus Golde will develop a bit of an eccentric reputation, but I couldn't care less.

What I really need is more time, I think. I know a good way to get that. "Your food is good," I tell her.

She flushes, a beautiful pink coloring her cheeks as she ducks her head slightly. Her chef coat is buttoned up to her throat, leaving me to wonder how far that blush goes, then scolding myself for the entirely inappropriate thought.

"You ever work as a private chef?" I ask.

"It's my day job," she admits.

"I'm new to town and trying to establish my day-to-day needs," I tell her, desperately clinging to whatever will get this woman to stay here with me. Although it's true—I'd be more than happy to eat this woman's food every day. "I'd like to hire you. Your food is good and I want more of it."

Her food is good, and I am looking for a chef. I was envisioning someone coming in two or three times a week, making a few things that I can just pop into the oven when I get hungry, but the vision suddenly changes. If I could have her in my house every day, then perhaps I could figure out why the dragon is clawing at me to be around her.

Dragons don't do that. I find humans amusing, at least most of the time, but the dragon couldn't care less about them. He's never demanded one's presence before.

Also by Addison James

<u>Supernatural Christmas</u>

A Recipe for Love

Snowed in with the Werewolf

<u>Crae Romance</u>

Callum

Bryce

Heath

Celia

Silas

Estrid

<u>Standalones</u>

Dragon's Treasure

The Heat Cure

About the author

Addison James is a romance book author from New England. They are obsessed with all things mythical, mystical, and magical. A lifelong fantasy reader, that evolved to fantasy romance as they grew up. Addison always has a story to tell and is excited to introduce you to their world of fantasy and paranormal romance.

You can find Addison at addyjameswriter.com, or by emailing them at addyjames@addyjameswriter.com.